# KNOT MY TYPE

## AN ALL ACCESS SERIES NOVEL

## EVIE MITCHELL

THUNDER THIGHS PUBLISHING

Editor: Nicole Wilson, Evermore Editing
http://www.evermoreediting.wixsite.com/info
Proofreading: Ashley Lewis, Geeky Girl Author Services
Eileen Widjaja, Cover Illustrator

 Created with Vellum

## ACKNOWLEDGEMENT OF COUNTRY

I acknowledge the Traditional Custodians of the lands on which I write, the Ngunnawal people, and pay my respect to elders both past and present.

I acknowledge the continued and deep spiritual relationship of the Australian Aboriginal and Torres Strait Islander peoples' to this land, and their unique cultural and spiritual relationships to the land, waters and seas and their rich contribution to society.

# BOOKS BY EVIE MITCHELL

**Capricorn Cove Series**

The Shake-Up

Double the D

Muffin Top

The Mrs. Clause

New Year Knew You

Double Breasted

As You Wish

You Sleigh Me

Meat Load

Resolution Revolution

**Larsson Sibling Series**

Thunder Thighs

Clean Sweep

The X-List

Reality Check

The Christmas Contract

**The Dogg Pack**

Puppy Love

Bad English

The Frock Up

Pier Pressure

**Nameless Souls MC Series**

Runner

Wrath

Ghost

Shield

**Elliot Security Series**

Rough Edge

Bleeding Edge

# CONNECT WITH EVIE MITCHELL

Facebook
Greedy Readers Book Club
TikTok
Instagram
Bookbub
Goodreads
Newsletter

*To Erin and Kirsten*
*Thank you for believing in this book and encouraging me to write*
*the stories of my heart.*
*You are the most amazing women ever.*

*And to my husband,*
*Do you want to try the cotton or the jute?*

# KNOT MY TYPE

**Frankie**

When you say you're a sexologist, people imagine Marilyn Monroe. They don't expect a woman who uses a wheelchair. As the host of the *All Access* podcast, I'm breaking barriers, crushing stigmas, and creating sexual connections that are fulfilling for my fans. I'm like cupid, but with pink hair and fewer diapers.

Only, I've hit a snag. A lovely listener wants some advice about accessible rope play and I'm drawing a big fat blank. Which leaves me with no option but to get out there and give it a go.

Which is how I meet Jay Wood—rigger, carpenter, and all-round hottie.

I'd be open to letting him wine and dine me but Jay isn't my type. He's not a one-girl kind of guy. Monogamy isn't even in his vocab, and I'm not a woman who'll settle for being second choice.

But the closer we get, the more Jay has me tied up in knots.

And it's making me think, maybe I could compromise

and accept a little Wood in my life. Even if it's only temporary.

**Jay**

Frankie's funny, intelligent, and ridiculously sexy. This should be a no-brainer. A little fun in the sheets, and a little romp with some ropes—simple.

Only the infuriating woman is asking for more. I'm not that kind of guy. I wouldn't even know how to be *that* kind of guy. I'm the definition of easy.

It'll be fine. We'll be friends. Just friends.

So, why does my heart feel frayed? And why is it I can't help but consider taking the ultimate leap of faith—tying myself to Frankie. Permanently.

# CONTENT WARNING AND TERMINOLOGY

This book contains references to foster care, and cheating in relationships, working with people who have experienced sexual trauma, and addiction.

There are graphic and very explicit descriptions of sex, kink, BDSM, rope play, binding, and spanking.

I acknowledge that shibari (or shibaru) is a general term in Japanese meaning "to tie." The correct Japanese term for the rope play in this book is kinbaku which refers to the weaving of intricate knots for binding and suspending people. Kinbaku is often considered to be an art form and is usually undertaken for pleasure. I chose to focus on this side of the practice, but because this book is set in my own fictional country which is based on Western culture, I have used shibari as that is the term recognised internationally.

The terms I use in the book are those taught to me by experienced riggers from Australia, the United States, and (formerly) Japan. The terminology top and bottom refer to the rope top or rigger (the person doing the tying) and the rope bottom (the person being tied).

I note that in some cultures top and bottom aren't used

in this way and dom/sub are preferred. While dom/sub can use shibari, the art of rope isn't limited to that relationship, hence the use of top/bottom.

While all care has been taken to ensure representation is respectful and inclusive, my sensitivity readers and my personal experience is limited to our own knowledge and understanding. If there is anything in the book that raises concerns for you, please feel free to reach out to EvieMitchel lAuthor@gmail.com.

Frankie

Today was a good day. No, it was what I liked to call a *best* day. The sort of day you'd remember weeks or months or years from now. The kind where at some point in the distant future you'd pull the memory from the dusty bookshelf in your mind, and still experience the same rush of emotion.

It was *that* kind of day.

One didn't generally wake up expecting to experience a best day. Save for weddings and births, best days weren't planned affairs. They just occurred, falling into your lap like little blessings sent from the gods.

In my life I'd now experienced a total of five best days. Being told I was cancer-free, my parents surprising my brother and I with a trip to Disneyland, receiving my doctorate, getting lost in Florence and discovering the best pastry shop in Italy, and now today.

I stared at the email, fingers trembling as I scrolled down the screen of my cell, reading the email for the fourth time.

Dear Dr. Kenton,

On behalf of the Association of Broadcasting, I am delighted to formally congratu-
late you on your nomination for a Poddie
Award for the *All Access* podcast.

*All Access* is an exemplar in inclusivity,
and your commitment to breaking down stigmas, changing perceptions, and challenging
thinking around sexuality and sex-posi-
tivity is to be commended.

We have enclosed the details of the nomination process and the awards festival.
Congratulations once again.

Sincerely,

*Luke Hamilton*

President
Association of Broadcasting

"A Poddie?" I asked, trembling. "I've been nominated for
an actual Poddie?"

My producer, Christine, nodded frantically. "And not
just any Poddie. Frankie, you've been nominated for *the*
Poddie."

I sucked in a breath, my hands pressing against my
cheeks. "Podcast of the Year?"

She nodded again, sending her riot of brunette hair
flying. "Along with—and babe, this is unheard of—Best

Production and Sound Design, Best Podcast Host, Best Knowledge, Science or Tech Podcast, Best Society and Culture Podcast, Best Wellness or Relationship Podcast, and Best Entertainment Podcast."

I sucked in a breath. "That's—" I quickly counted on my fingers. "Seven nominations. What the fuck? Seven, Christine? Seven!"

"I know!" My producer squealed, her hands rubbing together greedily. "Can you believe it? You're a fucking star, Frankie. This is our chance to take this baby to the next level."

"Talk show?" I asked, something fluttering wildly in my gut.

"Talk show," she confirmed, her expression looking distinctly sharkish. "Can you imagine? Your own talk show. Prime time. This has the potential to be huge for you."

I couldn't imagine. I couldn't even contemplate what my life might look like in that scenario.

"Let's not be too hasty," I said, scooting my wheelchair closer to the desk. "I mean, for all we know I might not even make it to the finals."

Chrissy snorted, rolling her eyes heavenward. "Babe, *no one* gets nominated for seven awards. Hell, the *Wicked Women* podcast only got two and they have a listenership of millions. You are *killing* this."

I tucked a stray chunk of pink hair behind my ear, my mind whirling.

"The next few weeks will be critical." She searched through the contents of her tote bag. "Where are the—ah! Found it." Withdrawing folded sheets, she smoothed out the papers to lay them on the desk between us.

"What's this?"

"The criteria for the competition. The judging takes

place over the next three months and includes a panel of five who will examine a sample of your episodes from the past year."

I frowned. "Why do I feel like there's a 'but' coming?"

"Not a 'but' so much as a 'be aware.'" Christine pointed to a highlighted passage. "The criteria for Podcast of the Year is rigorous. From the twenty-first they'll be listening to every episode you release in addition to the sample episodes we've submitted. The assessment criteria is top secret, but from my listen of the previous years' winners I'd say it's a combination of engaging content, consistency, and sparkle."

I chuckled. "Sparkle?"

Christine grinned. "Yep. The X-factor that sets you apart from the rest of the pack." She leaned in, her eyes twinkling. "And you, my dear Frankie-girl, have the spark."

I held up a hand for a high five. "Yeah, I do."

We slapped palms, both of us beaming.

"You worked hard for this Frankie. Be proud."

"It's all thanks to you."

Chrissy brushed my praise aside, but I caught her flash of pleasure.

I'd met Christine through a mutual friend at a party two years ago. Vibrant, larger than life, and hilarious, I'd been drawn to her like a moth to a flame. At the time, Chrissy had been single and contemplating IVF, bemoaning the state of the male dating pool, and on a rant about feminism and the power of single parents. Being what I liked to call an observer of human behaviour—translation, psychologist—I'd been obsessed with her and our conversation, both of us pounding red wine and talking late into the night.

As we'd rolled drunkenly out to our respective Ubers, Chrissy had handed me her card.

"If you ever feel like producing a podcast, call me."

I'd brushed off the suggestion, but a few months later over a frustration-laden video call with friends, the idea for the *All Access* podcast had been born—and Chrissy had loved it.

I refocused, moving the competition papers to the side of my desk and reaching for my notebook. "We'd better work out some kick-ass content for the next three months."

My lips curled into an amused grin. "And this is different to a regular week, how?"

Christine waved off my teasing. "We received a listener letter and it's one I want you to seriously consider." She delved back into her bag placing a pacifier, lactation cookies, and an apple on the desk before pulling an envelope free.

"Should I be scared?" I joked, accepting the letter.

"You tell me."

I scanned the contents, my eyes catching on three words. *Accessible rope play.*

"Well, this is unexpected," I murmured, rereading. "She wants help with shibari."

"You know it?"

I nodded then shook my head, shrugging. "No. Well, sort of. Maybe? I know *of* it—I've read about it and have some info about the theory but I haven't had any personal experience."

"Do you have any contacts who could help?"

I pursed my lips. "Not anyone I can think of. But I'll make some calls."

Christine leaned in. "I think we should spin this into at least a three-episode feature."

"Bondage?"

"Accessible bondage. This could be like the time you profiled the accessible sex toys and the podcast went viral."

I tilted my head to one side, grinning as I teased Christine. "Is this to help our listener or to win the Poddie?"

"Both. We can't win if we're not true to your listenership."

I sobered, once again grateful I'd chosen Christine as my agent and producer.

"You're right. Our values can't change." I looked down at the letter. "If she wants help with accessible rope play, we should go to the source—find a rigger who can help us."

"Rigger?"

"The name of someone who ties the ropes. They're the tops, bunnies or model are the bottoms."

"Well, I for one am already incredibly intrigued by what this feature might uncover." The engagement ring on her finger twinkled as she held her hand up. "And I'm sure my fiancé will be as well."

I rolled my eyes, throwing her a grin. "You selfish cow."

"You greedy goat."

We laughed, holding up coffee mugs in a toast to each other.

"To the *All Access* podcast."

"No, babe." She tipped her mug my way. "To you. And to your success. You deserve everything coming your way."

"I'll drink to that."

We clinked mugs and sipped, both of us savouring the rich coffee.

"Now." Christine set her cup aside, opening her laptop. "Let's get planning. We have a show to run and awards to win."

I took a moment to file away every part of this best day.

With a grin, I nodded. "Alright. Let's win this thing."

## 2

Frankie

I watched the crackle and pop of the fire, gently turning my marshmallow until the skin began to bubble and brown. With practiced ease, I slid the treat off my stick, enjoying the explosion of warmed sugar on my tongue.

My brother had outdone himself this time. Between the homemade marshmallows, and the delicious ribs and sides already sitting in my belly, this had to be one of the best feasts we'd had in a while. Certainly better than last week when I'd been forced to serve toast after burning the lasagna.

Friday night feasts were an institution amongst our friendship group, and Noah took it as a personal challenge to exceed expectations every time. I both loved and hated that he'd managed to absorb all of our dad's cooking genes.

"Oh, shit," Annie whispered, stiffening beside me. "He's here."

Seated around the backyard fire pit were my closest

friends—Annie, Florence, and Mai. We'd been joined at the hip since high school—having met in a bathroom after eating bad cafeteria pizza. Despite college, jobs, and distance, we'd remained friends through thick and thin—and somehow made our way back to Capricorn Cove.

I glanced over to find Annie glaring at the man standing next to my brother at the buffet table.

"Annie." Mai's tawny cheeks flushed with annoyance. "He's friends with Noah. Lincoln attends every event. You need to get over it."

My brother stood in profile, his shock of dark brown hair standing on all ends. My fingers itched to smooth it out as he chatted with the latecomer. Lincoln clapped my brother on his shoulder, gesturing at the feast Noah had laid out. Tall, broad, and full of fire, Lincoln had once been the dark contrast to Annie's sunshine glow. These days, those roles seemed to have reversed.

*I will not involve myself in my friend's affairs. I will not involve myself in my friend's affairs. I will not—*

Annie flicked Mai an annoyed look, her golden eyes flashing in the firelight. "I *know*. It doesn't mean I have to like it though."

I popped another marshmallow on my stick, determined to avoid this conversation.

My friends were a comedy of contrasts. There was tall, curvy, dramatic Annie with her cascade of blonde hair and golden eyes. The prankster amongst us, she prickled and poked, flowing from high maintenance to sarcastic in one breath. Under her tough exterior beat a vulnerable heart that loved fiercely.

Annie owned S#!T Happens, a subscription toilet paper company she'd started during college. Tired of having to trek out to the store when sick, she'd started the company on the back of a toilet paper roll while experiencing a Crohn's flare-up. I'd never been more proud.

Flo stood behind her, weaving ribbon into Annie's hair. Average height with long brunette hair and delicate features, we often joked Flo should have been born a princess since all she lacked was a prince to sweep her away. She believed in romance and abundant optimism; her every action aimed at bettering the world through loving kindness. If I could aspire to be anyone, it would be Flo.

Mai sat beside them nursing a beer. Short and plump with ebony hair that tended to be a riot of misplaced strands, Mai strode through life with her head up and heart out, demonstrating a fierce frankness I admired. She had the kind of drive and determination that pushed her to excel at her craft, designing fabric prints that sold all over the world. But her true love lay in sustainable design. I owned a wardrobe filled with Mai originals. I couldn't wait for her to step out of the shadows and into the fashion world.

I watched as her fingers—stained with red dye— absently picked at the label of her beer.

"Are we talking about Linc again?" Flo asked. Her free hand searched for her chair, her other gripping the handle of Ace, her guide dog's, harness.

"Yeah." Mai rolled her eyes, tucking a strand of short dark hair behind her ear. "Annie's in a mood."

"I am not," Annie retorted, tossing her braid. "I'm just saying he could be more considerate."

I rolled my eyes, blowing on my now browned dessert before popping it in my mouth.

Flo removed a beer bottle from her dress pocket, twisting off the cap. "How? It's a small town and you've been separated since high school. Surely you should be over him by now."

Annie crossed her arms over her ample chest, her lips pressing into a pout.

"She's pouting, isn't she?" Flo asked humour in her tone.

Annie blew a raspberry her way. "Shut up, Miss-Know-It-All."

"You shut up, Miss-Woe-Is-Me."

"By the way, are you wearing a new perfume?" Annie asked her, lifting her braid to her nose for a sniff. "I now smell like... flowers?"

"Actually, it's lime, orange blossom, and a hint of liquorice. I think it will be the signature aroma for Common Scents' fall line."

Flo had opened her apothecary the year prior. Specialising in custom natural products, her perfumes, candles, and aromatherapy lines had become something of an online hit.

"I'd buy it."

Mai laughed, shaking her head. "You'd buy anything we produce."

Annie grinned, lifting her beer in silent salute. "As a good friend should."

I rolled my eyes. "Would you all be quiet for a second? I have something I need help with."

"Is it another podcast episode?" Mai asked, leaning forward. "'Cause I have ideas."

"Like?" Flo asked her.

"I thought she could do a piece on body art. There's this woman I know who—"

"Hey." I shut down the conversation knowing this could rapidly spiral out of control if I wasn't careful. "The rest of you can wait. Though I do want to hear more about the body art later. This is serious—I need to find someone experienced with BDSM. Or, more precisely, rope play."

There was a beat of silence.

"Rope play?" Flo asked, her fingers scratching Ace's head. "What does that mean?"

"It's when someone ties you up," Annie said, a small frown marring her forehead. "They call it something else though."

"Shibari." I cocked an eyebrow at my friend. "Do you know someone?"

Annie's gaze flicked toward Linc but she shook her head slowly. "Not personally. Not for sure but I've heard of someone."

"Who?"

"Jay Wood."

"As in the guy we went to school with?" Flo asked, tilting her head to one side, her fancy sunglasses reflecting the firelight.

"Yeah, you remember him?"

"Vaguely." I searched my memory trying to conjure his face. "Is he related to the Dogg family in some way?"

"Foster kid. Aged out but stuck around. He works at Dogg Wood Lumber with his former foster dad. I think he's a carpenter as well."

"How do you know all this?" Flo asked Annie, as she lifted her beer to her lips. "Are you moonlighting as a PI?"

Annie chuckled. "I make it my job to know about the single men in this town."

"And he's into rope?" I asked, bringing the conversation back around.

"That I can't confirm. But I have heard he does classes at The A-List."

Mai sucked in a breath. "The kink club?"

Annie nodded. "Yep. Jay's probably your best bet, Frankie."

I frowned. "But how? I mean do I call him at work and say, 'Hey, we went to school together a million years ago and now I want to pick your brain about BDSM'?"

Flo snorted, beer spurting out her nose. I thrust napkins into her hands, chuckling at her mess.

"Sorry," she said, mopping at the fizz. "It's just—can you imagine? What if he had you on loudspeaker?"

I grinned. "But seriously, any ideas?"

Mai raised a hand. "Actually, yeah. Ren might have his number. I think they play basketball together on Wednesdays."

I stared at her. "Babe, I could kiss you. Actually, scratch that. I could kiss your brother."

She laughed. "You say that but we all know he'd die of embarrassment."

"Where is your brother?" Flo asked. "I haven't heard him tonight."

"Somewhere around here. I expect he's trying to avoid Brooklyn. I heard she's back on the prowl."

Annie snorted. "Is she still trying to hook him?"

"Uh-huh." Mai sighed. "I wish he'd give in. Between him and Keiko, I'm never going to become the cool drunk aunt."

I laughed at the picture of one-drink-and-she's-dancing-on-the-table Mai sipping vodka and doling out sassy wisdom to a packet of nieces and nephews.

"I don't," Flo said. "Brooklyn's not right for him."

I put my hands on my push rims, backing up. "As fun as this conversation is, let me get Jay's number before we begin matchmaking. You guys need anything?"

They shook their heads.

I narrowed my gaze on Mai. "Don't eat all the marsh-mallows."

She stuck her tongue out at me. "No promises."

With a laugh, I flicked her the bird, wheeling away from the fire to search the party for Ren.

Noah had purchased his house a few years ago, spending most weekends restoring the old lady to her current grand glory. Pictures hung on the walls, moody black-and-white images taken around Capricorn Cove and during his overseas travels, each more beautiful than the last.

*He really should do this full-time. His art is too powerful to hide away.*

I moved down the hall, peeking into rooms searching for Ren.

"Frankie?" Noah stopped me in the hall.

"Hey, you seen Ren?"

"In the den with the boys." He jerked his thumb behind him. "You need a hand with something?"

"Nope, just have a question for Ren. Thanks." I adjusted my chair, moving to wheel past him.

"We still on for dinner this week?"

I laughed, shooting him a look over my shoulder. "You're really getting desperate if you need to beg for dates from your sister."

"After the last disaster, I'd say you're the safer bet."

His date had managed to get stupidly drunk and end the night by vomiting on Noah's best shoes. Despite the guy apologising, there hadn't been a second date.

I threw him a wink. "You're on, but you're also buying dessert."

I found Ren in the den, nursing a beer. A baseball game played on the large screen TV as the gathered group watched in rapt attention.

I waited for a break before pushing into the room, Ren spotting me immediately.

"Hey, Lanky Frankie." Ren grinned, waving me over. "Want a beer?"

During my teen years, I'd briefly nursed a crush on Ren Sakamoto, dreaming he'd kiss me with those beautiful lips, and wrap me in his long, strong arms as I ran fingers through his inky hair.

My crush had quickly passed when I'd discovered the powerful pull of rock stars and leading men, but my fondness for him would never die. If you looked up 'good guy' on Google, Ren's picture would appear.

Seriously, Annie had set up a website in his honour. We still couldn't figure out how she'd made it the top suggestion, but there it remained.

I shook my head. "I'm good. Just after a favour."

"Shoot."

"Do you have Jay Wood's number?"

Ren nodded, reaching for his cell. "You after some lumber?"

I swallowed a giggle at his unintended innuendo. "Something like that."

He rattled off the numbers as I pressed them into my cell.

"You want me to—"

The crowded room surged to their feet, shouting at the TV as beers and popcorn flew through the air.

"And I'm out." I wheeled backward shooting a grin at Ren. "Thanks for the help."

"Anytime." He'd already turned back to the screen, his expression outraged as he caught the replay. "What the fuck?"

In the dark hall, I paused, my fingers hovering over the screen of my cell.

*Am I really doing this?*

I sucked in a breath, quickly tapping out a message.

FRANKIE

> Hi Jay, this is Frankie Kenton. Sorry for the random text but I heard you might know something about accessible rope play and/or BDSM. Could we catch up for coffee this week to talk? Thanks!

I considered adding an emoji—torn between an eggplant, a smiley face, or a love heart.

"Stop it. An emoji would be far too weird." Before I could talk myself out of it, I hit send.

"Well hell," I muttered, sucking in a breath in an attempt to calm my pounding heart. "Either this is going to win me a Poddie or I've needlessly creeped a guy out."

With a long, hard sigh, I returned to the fire and the now-empty container of marshmallows.

# 3

---

**Jay**

Sprawled out on my sofa, I stared blankly at the ball game, a half-drunk beer balanced precariously on my stomach.

*This is exactly how I wanted to spend my Friday night —alone.*

It'd been brewing for a while but I'd finally succumbed to my dreaded malaise. I had offers of parties, offers of hookups, offers of fun, and yet here I lay—staring at a game I didn't care about, drinking a beer I didn't enjoy, while I filled my stomach with my least favourite flavour of potato chip.

"I should order a pizza."

Saying it aloud didn't change the reality—there'd be no pizza for Jay Wood tonight. I couldn't summon the effort.

I'd experienced these kinds of dips my whole life. Ennui. Listlessness. The words all meant the same thing—I needed a change. That was the problem with being me, I bored easily. My foster dad had called me a minute man—always searching for the next thing. My brothers gave me shit about the name but it fit. And lately, nothing piqued my interest.

"Maybe I need a vacation."

Even saying the words aloud didn't inspire a flicker of curiosity.

"Or I could lay here until the Goddess of Interesting Things sends something my way."

As if hearing my plea, my cell chirped, notifying me of a text.

I took a long drag of my beer, summoning the energy to pull it from my back pocket.

*Look at me being a successful human being. I moved a whole three inches.*

Chuckling darkly, I glanced at the screen.

UNKNOWN NUMBER.

"Huh."

I swiped to open, reading the message, my eyebrows rising in mild surprise.

UNKNOWN NUMBER

> Hi Jay, this is Frankie Kenton. Sorry for the random text but I heard you might know something about accessible rope play and/or BDSM. Could we catch up for coffee this week to talk? Thanks!

"Well." I crunched up into a seated position, rereading the text. "This is unexpected."

I took another sip as I considered the text.

Frankie Kenton. I knew the name but couldn't quite place the face.

"Time for some light social media stalking."

It took me less than three minutes to track down little Ms. Kenton. That was the beauty of a small town, everyone knew or knew of everyone else—perfect for the mature sleuth.

I found her Instagram page, clicking on the little icon to scope her out.

"Well, hello." Her profile had me smiling.

> *Frankie Kenton*
> *She/Her/Dr.*
> *Avoider of conflicts*
> *Absolute disaster in the kitchen*
> *Host of the* All Access *podcast*
> *Certified Sexologist*

My fingers slid down the screen, stopping on the most recent picture in her grid. The caption read

Pink hair don't care. #LaughLikeYouMeanIt

I found myself smiling at the utter joy in her expression. Head tilted back, pink hair wild, blue eyes sparkling, she made me feel something I hadn't in a while.

Interest.

I continued to scroll, enjoying the colour and laughter in her pictures.

"Alright, Frankie. You've got my attention."

I took a long draw of my beer, contemplating my move.

In my world there were only two reasons people text you out of the blue—they either wanted something, or you owed them something.

"Fuck it, I'm willing to roll the dice."

I took another swig before hitting reply.

JAY

Hi Frankie, I have to admit, you've caught my interest. I can definitely meet for coffee. Would tomorrow work?

I hit send, pushing to my feet to get another beer, and ordering a pizza as I waited for her reply.

Tight with anticipation, I paced, the pizza arriving before I received her response.

FRANKIE

Tomorrow is great. Should we try Books and Beans?

JAY

Sounds good. 10ish work for you?

FRANKIE

Perfect. I'll be the one wearing the pink wheelchair ;)

I grinned, shooting her a reply. I leaned against my kitchen island, tearing off a bite of pepperoni pizza while I waited.

JAY

I'll be the hot guy with the Lego tattoos.

FRANKIE

LOL! Now those I *have* to see.

I chewed slowly considering if I should send her back something flirty.

"This is the most interest you've shown in months," I reminded myself, playing devil's advocate. "How about you savour this? We both know it isn't gonna last."

Satisfied, I ended our conversation with a promise.

JAY

I'll see you tomorrow.

FRANKIE

Yep! Looking forward to it.

I lifted a second piece from the box, rereading her message as I finished the slice.

"You know, surprisingly, so am I."

**Jay**

Capricorn Cove had experienced a renaissance in the last few years, the sleepy town beginning to emerge from its hibernation as people moved in, and businesses finally occupied formerly vacant storefronts.

Change came slowly in the Cove, but Books and Beans had fast become a local institution.

Inside the small café, warm brick walls were complemented by polished concrete floors, long wood benches, and up-cycled tables. Bookshelves stuffed with new and used books were scattered throughout the space, inviting diners to peruse as they waited for their order.

I pushed through the door, the bell tinkling cheerfully above my head.

"Hey, Jay. Want your regular?" Betsy called from her position behind the counter. Dressed in a casual blouse and mom-jeans, the older woman didn't look like the kind of person who'd own a hipster joint. And yet, a quick glance around showed a surprising number of tourists enjoying generous meals.

"Actually, I'm meeting someone. Got a table for me?"

She nodded toward the back of the café indicating a table set between the currently empty fireplace and a pair of wall-to-ceiling bookshelves.

"Perfect. Thanks."

I made my way over, calling greetings and stopping for chats with locals. That was the problem with a small town— you knew everyone and everyone knew you.

Everyone, it seemed, except Frankie Kenton.

I settled at the table, anticipation simmering under my skin as I pulled my cell out, swiping to reread her messages.

I still couldn't figure out why she'd piqued my interest. There was nothing profound in her texts. And yet here I sat, waiting for her to arrive, my pulse unsteady, my body on edge.

*What the fuck is wrong with me?*

"Jay?"

I looked up to catch sight of the woman pushing toward me, feeling as if I'd been sucker punched.

*Holy shit.*

"Frankie?"

Her pink hair and blue eyes reminded me of the cotton candy I used to buy at the annual fair. The colours had me wondering if the taste of her promised to be as sweet on my tongue.

She grinned, her eyes sparkling as she held out a hand. "The one and only."

I'd have classified her as spun sugar, light and fluffy and extra sweet—if not for her voice. The richness of it forced me to reassess my initial impression—this woman wasn't sugar, she was spice in masquerade.

*Now I want chocolate. These food comparisons are getting out of hand.*

I slid my palm against hers, feeling the worn calluses and strong grip of her hand.

"Jay Wood." I gestured at the table I'd picked. "This okay?"

"Perfect."

She moved a chair out of her way to scoot into place, watching me with a mysterious little smile.

I liked her boldness, her gaze locking with mine as we ignored the bustling brunch crowd around us.

If I'd been asked to describe her, I'd say a riot of colour. From her pink wheelchair and sky-blue nails to the pastel watercolour leggings and pink knee-high boots, she didn't strike me as ordinary. Her shirt read *Here for the rolls* with an image of a wheelchair doing a wheelie, and I could imagine her attempting the same stunt, pink hair caught in the breeze, laughter on her lips.

*Where the hell are these thoughts coming from?*

"You're not what I imagined," Frankie broke our silence.

Her quiet admission had me grinning. "No?"

She shook her head, tendrils of pink hair gently floating with the movement. "Not at all."

"What were you expecting?"

She grinned, her eyes sparkling. "Less lumbersexual and more Christian Grey perhaps?"

I laughed, already enjoying this conversation far more than I'd enjoyed anything in months. "Who says I don't have a secret sex room ready for debauchery?"

Frankie laughed and I found myself captivated by her unfiltered reaction. Maybe I'd become jaded, but lately I'd spent far too many hours dealing with people who only presented what they wanted you to see. Her lack of artifice felt like a breath of fresh air and left me aching to know more.

*Jesus, man, settle the fuck down. You've just met her.*

"Coffee?" Betsy appeared at our table, her wrinkled face a wreath of smiles as her gaze danced between us. "Our special today is pancakes with cream, ice cream, and berries."

"Done," Frankie declared. "And a large cappuccino please."

Betsy made a note and then looked at me.

"Pancakes as well but add some bacon. And I'll take a long black. Thanks, Betsy."

"Great, it'll be ready soon."

"Sorry," Frankie said, giving me a lopsided smile. "I didn't even ask if you wanted food."

"I'm a single guy whose housemate abandoned him for married life. I always want food—especially if I'm not cooking it."

She grinned then sobered, one hand raising to tuck a chunk of hair behind her ears. "I'm sure you're wondering why I texted you."

"A little," I admitted, leaning my forearms on the table. "And how you got my number."

"Ren gave it to me. I'm best friends with Mai."

Betsy returned, setting our drinks down before scurrying off to serve a cranky woman at the counter.

I cupped my mug, catching Frankie's gaze. "That explains the how but not the why. What do you think I can help with?"

A flush worked its way up her neck. "I'm a sexologist and I run the *All Access* podcast. Have you heard of it?"

I shook my head.

"It's a bi-weekly podcast where I profile different accessibility issues. Part of my show focuses on sex, but a lot of it is about encouraging conversations and learning more about people."

"That's cool."

"Thanks." She grinned. "I really enjoy giving back, and my listenership are the best." She reached into her bag to pull an envelope free. "I have a segment where listeners can write in and I answer their questions. Most of the time the letters are issues I can help with—sex toys, psychological concerns, different supports. But this one threw me."

She slid the paper across the table. "I redacted their personal information but kept the relevant parts."

I skimmed the letter, surprised to find myself disappointed that this coffee meeting wasn't for her own interest.

"I can help." I handed her back the written request. "But explaining rope play is different to experiencing it."

Frankie nodded, her lips pursing. "I expected as much. Do you do much with accessibility?" She tapped a blue-tipped finger to the letter. "This person has very specific questions."

"I can answer all those questions, but you might find it more useful to attend one of my classes."

"Classes?"

"I run an accessible bondage class at The A-List once a month."

Frankie's eyebrows rose slightly. "That's the kink club, right?"

I nodded, taking a sip of my coffee, my leg jiggling under the table.

When I told people I taught kink, the typical reactions fell somewhere between revulsion, embarrassment, or sexual interest. Frankie surprised me by taking a sip of her coffee, her expression curious.

"How did you get started?"

Betsy reappeared, two steaming plates of pancakes in hand.

"Here you go." She slid them onto the table, handing over cutlery. "You need anything else?"

We shook our heads.

"Great, call if you do."

I paused, fork raised as I watched Frankie scoop a giant spoonful of cream from the top of her pancake pile. Her tongue flicked out, capturing the fluffy white dollop.

My cock hardened, my body rigid as I watched her eyelids drift shut, listening to the satisfied moan as she savoured the taste.

I found myself wondering if she'd make the same sound when I got her under me, my mouth on her—

She sighed, stabbing at a slice of pancake. "I love brunch."

"So do I."

I shifted in my seat, grimacing at the press of my cock against my zipper.

*I haven't had to deal with a reaction like this since high school. Pull it together man!*

"Where were we?" I asked, desperate to change the subject.

"How you got started in bondage."

*Well fuck.*

"Right. Of course." I sucked in a breath. "It's a pretty basic story. Guy's friend goes to college. Friend asks guy to look in on his mom while he's away. Guy finds mom is a cougar. Cougar teaches him some interesting techniques. Cougar and guy break up. Guy travels the world. Guy watches a shibari session and ends up practising the art."

Frankie's fork hovered near her lips, a low and melodic giggle escaping her.

*Fuck, she even laughs sexy.*

"That's a basic story?"

I grinned, reaching for the maple syrup. "Well, for me it is."

"Okay, I have questions. As an avid romance reader, I need to know—what was she like, how old, who is she, how did you meet, why did you break up?"

I forced a laugh, tipping the syrup bottle to smother my meal. "I was maybe twenty-one? She was mid-forties, newly divorced and the mom of a friend."

"Oh, my God!" Frankie's cutlery clattered to the table as her hands pressed against her chest. "Tell me ev-er-y-thing!"

"Not much to say except she made the first move, I found her hot AF and we were together for a little over a year."

"Did your friend know?"

I shook my head. "Fuck no. He would have killed me."

"Didn't stop you."

I watched her take a sip of her coffee. "At the time the threat added to the spice."

She snorted, coughing. "Oh my God, Jay!"

I shoved napkins at her, amused by her antics. "Sorry, not sorry."

She cleaned herself up, shaking her head. "Just for that, you have to tell me more."

I scratched my chin trying to work out how to change the subject. "She broke up with me. I left for a two-year backpacking trip, and later heard she slept with half of my friend's graduating class."

"Power to her," Frankie said, looking impressed. "She must have been something."

"She was."

"So she helped you discover kink?"

"Tangentially. I backpacked my way around Europe, stumbling into the scene along the way. She helped me work out what I wanted from sexual partners and how to pleasure them, but those clubs taught me that what I like isn't shameful or wrong just because it's different."

Frankie nodded. "I agree. It's why I became a sexologist."

My eyebrows rose. "Because of kink?"

She shook her head. "No, because of shame. Back in school, we had a sex education class. It was a regular occurrence every year but this time they were talking about reproduction. The teacher asked me to leave. When I asked why, he said I didn't need to know this because I'd never have a sexual relationship." Her cheeks flushed, her blue eyes flashing with fire. "I told him where he could shove his sexist, ableist bullshit."

I lifted a hand for a high five. "You go girl."

She slapped it but shook her head again. "When people think of a sexologist, they assume I'll be someone super sexual —like Marilyn Monroe or a porn star. But first and foremost, I'm a doctor of the brain. I'm not there to get them off, but to coach people through their insecurities and fears. Many of the clients I work with are survivors of sexual trauma. My job is to help them find the confidence to reclaim their sexuality."

"I must admit to some social media stalking and saw you're Doctor Kenton."

She grinned. "I like that you admit you stalked me."

"Only the publicly available stuff. I save the hacking for date three."

She laughed, scraping her fork across her plate to collect the last crumbs of pancake and cream. "Now, about this rope stuff?"

*Don't tell her anything.*

The thought rattled me, but watching her lick her fork clean, I realised our time might be coming to an end, and there might be a possibility I'd expired my usefulness.

For reasons I had yet to understand, I wanted to keep her sapphire gaze locked on me for longer than this brief brunch meeting.

"Come to the club," I blurted out. "I'm teaching next Saturday."

Frankie's brows rose. "You want me to come to a class?"

"Yeah. You can see what I do." A devil sat on my shoulder, whispering in my ear. "Or, if you want, you could be the demonstration model."

"You want to tie me up?"

"Only if you're into it."

Her cheeks flushed, her gaze dropping to her plate before determinedly rising. "I guess it would be hypocritical for me to do a podcast about accessible bondage and rope play without actually experiencing it."

"It's clothes on," I rushed to assure her, my heart doing a weird ticktack in my chest. "No nudity for the class."

"Alright," Frankie said slowly. "What do I wear?"

"Comfortable clothing. No bra."

Her eyebrows rose but she didn't question me.

"What time?"

"I'll text you the details." I pretended to glance at my watch, swearing softly. "Shit, is that the time? I've got to run." I rose, pulling my wallet free to drop enough cash to cover our meals and a tip for Betsy.

I leaned down intending to press a quick kiss to her warm cheek, but her soft skin invited my lips to linger, the strands of her hair caressing my cheek in welcome.

*Fuck. Pull it together, Jay! Get the fuck out of here before she changes her mind.*

I jerked upright, shooting her a grin I knew didn't quite reach my eyes. "See you next week, Frankie. It has been an absolute pleasure."

She stammered out a farewell, her gaze boring a hole in my back as I exited the café, leaving behind the most intriguing woman I'd met in years.

*Well, I'm certainly not bored anymore.*

# 5

***

### Frankie

My fingers gripped the cool metal of my push rims as I attempted to summon my courage. The nondescript building seemed to taunt me, whispering doubts into my mind.

"Francine Ursula Charles Kenton," I muttered, forcing my shoulders back. "You're a grown woman with sexual desires. What would you say to your clients if they were worried about attending a sex club?"

I laughed at my own hesitancy. "Get your ass in there!"

My cell buzzed, alerting me to the fifth notification in thirty seconds. With a sigh, I pulled it free, swiping to read.

MAI

Are you there yet?

ANNIE

Girl, you are the BEST! I can't wait to hear about this adventure!

FLO

> Ask about sensory play. And if they have a
> candle distributor. I'd assume they have
> candle needs?

I chuckled, shaking my head at her question.

ANNIE

> Always with the hustle, Flo. We really need
> to find you a man.

MAI

> Wait. She gets a man because she's
> hustling? Does that mean we need to get
> you two, Annie?

ANNIE

> THIS ISN'T ABOUT ME! IT'S ABOUT
> FRANKIE! Frankie, you better not be
> replying because you're inside the club and
> not because you chickened out.

I tapped out a quick reply before switching my cell off, dropping it back in my bag.

FRANKIE

> I just arrived. Heading in now. Wish me luck!

Determined, I lifted my chin, straightened in my chair and pushed forward, shifting to hit the button for the intercom on the side of the building.

"Hello?" a feminine voice asked.

*You got this, Frankie.*

"Hi," I chirped, my voice strangely high-pitched. "This is Frankie. I'm here for the rope class?"

"Oh, hey, doll! Jay said you'd be coming. I'll buzz the door. We're in the green room, you can't miss it."

There was a small beep, the automatic door inching open to grant me entrance to the club.

"No turning back now."

I made my way down a small entrance corridor following discreet signs advising the class would be held in a room at the rear of the big building.

Capricorn Cove wasn't the kind of place you'd expect to find a BDSM club. The small-town coastal village didn't exactly scream kink-inclusive. But a few decades back the area had been home to a free-love hippy commune. While the hippies were long gone and the commune had been revamped into an upscale resort, the love-acceptance vibe remained.

It was one of the reasons I'd chosen to return to the Cove after receiving my PhD. Well, that and Noah—but he was a whole other story.

"You must be Frankie." A woman dressed in latex stepped out of a doorway to my right, her hand outstretched. "I'm Lea."

I shook her hand, attempting not to stare at her wealth of bosom as it threatened to spill from her suit. "Hey. Sorry I'm late. It took me a minute to find the place."

She made a dismissive gesture. "You're right on time. We're still waiting on Jay to finish setting up. Do you want a quick tour?"

I nodded, anticipation uncurling in my belly as she led me through the premise.

"Jay mentioned you're a sexologist?"

I nodded.

"This must be pretty vanilla to you," she said, sweeping a hand out to encompass the building.

"You'd think so but absolutely not. My clinical work specialises in relationship counselling and trauma. While being open and talking about play is an important part of my sessions, the clients I see aren't normally looking for help with kink so much as figuring out where to even start with sex. A lot of my clients have experienced trauma or live with medical conditions that make intimacy difficult."

Lea nodded, hitting a button to open a door to one of the rooms. "Must feel like you've won the jackpot when someone overcomes one of their barriers."

I chuckled. "Successes should always be celebrated." I glanced around, noting the equipment in the room. "What's this one?"

"It's our massage room. Particularly popular among the parents in our club."

She walked me through the building explaining the different rooms, how the club operated, and giving me a rundown of the rules—spoken and unspoken. She provided a fascinating insight into kink culture; her passion for inclusive play clear to see.

"You know, I have to admit to having some preconceived ideas before coming here."

Lea laughed. "Everyone does. It's why we started the classes. Some people want to step outside their comfort zones but without an audience. If they're not taught how to play safely and with consent then things start to go wrong."

I nodded. "That's what I tell people in my practice—consent, safety, and trust. If you can't communicate what you want then it's not going to be a fun time for anyone."

Lea shot me a grin. "Exactly." She pushed the final door open, holding it while I wheeled through. "Looks like Jay's ready for us."

Ropes hung from hooks in the ceilings and walls, the white lengths a stark contrast to the dark green of the walls.

*No doubt a purposeful decision.*

The mostly empty room held ropes, a few temporary curtained cubicles on the far left wall, and a small number of chairs that were positioned around gym mats in the centre of the space. Couples sat waiting for class to begin, their soft murmured conversations the only sound in the big space.

My attention snagged on Jay as he stood in the middle of the room, running a length of rope absently across his palm. Average height, lean but ruggedly muscular, the man's unruly dark brown hair seemed at odds with his short, well-kept beard. A plethora of colourful tattoos covered one of his well-built arms, the Lego figures shifting in time with his movements.

*How is he more attractive here than at brunch?*

"We ready?" he asked, his deep voice cutting through the quiet.

"Yep. This is the last one," Lea answered, gesturing for me to join the other students.

I coasted forward, stopping next to a woman and her partner, both of them looking equal parts nervous and excited.

*I feel the exact same way.*

"Great." Jay turned to the students, one hand shoving a flop of messy dark hair out of his eyes. "Welcome to Accessible Bondage 101. In this class, you'll learn the building blocks of accessible bondage, including its history, basics, safety, and a few ties to get you started at home." He glanced around the room, his green gaze piercing as he considered us. "This is a fully accessible class—if there's anything that doesn't feel good or any way we can assist you to feel more safe, comfortable or included please let Lea or myself know."

For a moment our eyes locked, holding. As I watched, his lips quirked, a slow knowing grin stretching across his too handsome face.

Red flags began to wave while warning lights flashed in my brain.

*Uh-oh. I think Jay might be a bad boy.*

"Alright," he said, gaze still locked with mine. "Let's begin."

**Jay**

Fuck she's sexy.

I watched Frankie as I explained the history of rope play and the terminology used in Western kink.

With her big sapphire eyes, full generous lips, and curvy breasts, in this setting she reminded me of a pinup girl, all generous curves and knowing looks. She brought to mind a rainbow with her pastel yellow shirt, and comfortable-looking blue pants, the pink shade of her shoes matching her wheelchair, nail polish and long hair.

All week I'd been on edge expecting a text from her declining my offer. With every notification, I'd reached for my cell dreading the possibility of seeing those three words on the screen—*I can't come.*

Seeing her now, I relaxed, the anxious tension releasing while a new awareness took its place.

*Focus.*

I forced my gaze away from the intriguing Frankie, to

survey the rest of the class. A few new couples, a few returning couples, and one thruple who'd been attending various classes the last few months. All looked eager to be here.

I breathed out a silent sigh, grateful there weren't likely to be any wannabe doms in this group. I didn't need Frankie's first time marred by some jerk thinking he knew better.

"The reason we use, and teach rope use in this class," I explained, "is because it's more adaptable to different needs. If you want to try cuffs, or leather, or other forms of restraints, have at it. But I'd suggest starting slow and working up."

I lifted a short length of rope, considering the assembled class. Each time I taught I reworked the lesson on the fly, ensuring I covered the different accessibility needs of my students.

"Now, rope choice is often down to the rigger but when engaging in accessible play, it might be up to the bunny to choose." I passed around the jute sample. "It's something that should be negotiated before a scene begins. Like I said earlier, open communication, discussion of where to touch and where not to, sensual levels, sexual touch, and even rope type should be considered. You want this to be a positive experience for everyone."

I lifted a piece of white cotton rope from my sample box, holding it up. "For example, if your partner has sensory sensitivities, cotton might be a better option as it's soft on the skin and tends to be gentle when bound. It also doesn't have much of a smell. If you're someone who wants to engage all senses, hemp might be better as it has a very unique smell. You should also consider burn rate when choosing rope, friction is important as you might or might not want to mark the bunny's skin."

A bark of laughter from one of the women in the group had me grinning. There was always one who found the bunny reference amusing.

*You'll learn.*

I held up a coloured cord. "You can use different coloured nylon to achieve different results. For example—"

"Young man," Mel, one of our regulars, interrupted me. "I don't want to stop you, but will we be getting to the ties soon? I'm not getting any younger."

Melissa and Norm couldn't be a day under seventy. They lived in Capricorn Cove and had reportedly been a part of the free-love commune that had lived here back in the late-sixties. Together they'd raised six kids, and had eight grand-kids and counting. They'd been attending the accessible classes since Norm's stroke two years ago. Dressed in full leopard print with wild orange hair, Mel regularly inter-rupted to demand less theory and more action in my classes.

I laughed. "Thanks for the prompt, Mel. Let me finish off on why rope is important, and some of the safety concerns and issues you'll want to try to prevent—like rope burn. Then we'll get to the good stuff."

I ran through some of the things to watch for and handed out pairs of rope cutting shears.

"Always," I emphasised, binding Lea's wrists in a quick knot. "Have these on hand. If for any reason you need to get your bunny out of a bind, this is the quickest way."

Lea positioned herself toward the audience, allowing me to demonstrate how to safely cut the rope for removal.

"Alright, any questions?"

The class shook their heads.

"Great. Let's get to the fun part."

I turned to the rainbow in the room.

"Frankie, are you happy to help me with this scene?"

I watched her cheeks flush, enjoying the colour I'd added to her already beautiful canvas.

She nodded. "Sure."

As Frankie pushed forward, her long pink hair swaying, I met her nervous gaze, something jumping between us.

*This was a terrible idea.*

I didn't know this woman. I didn't know what she might be like in a scene. She could freak out. She could lose herself. She could do any number of things which would result in a bad experience.

*This was a stupid fucking idea. I need to stop thinking with my fucking dick.*

Her chair stopped at the edge of the mat, her gaze questioning. For a beat I watched her, considering options, acting as if I hadn't thought constantly about this moment for the last week.

*Approach this the way you would any other scene—from the beginning.*

"We're going to walk through the things I need to know, and which Frankie wants me to know, before we get started. Like I've said, before you begin a scene understanding how to engage in safe, consensual, enjoyable play is essential. Here at the club, we call it the A-List."

"A-list?" Frankie asked, raising an eyebrow, a small smile playing on her ruby red lips.

"Answer list. Or access list. However you want to describe it, it's essential to a good scene."

Lea dimmed the room lights until a single circle illuminated the mats, the rest of the room in shadow.

"So, Frankie," I said, beginning the negotiation. "Would you prefer to use your chair during scenes?"

She hesitated, her fingers flexing. "What are my options if I don't?"

I gestured at Lea. "In a scenario where people prefer not to use their equipment, we get them onto the floor or a soft surface. You want a place where people are less likely to injure themselves if they fall. In this scenario, we'd ask you to start on the mats. Lea would be the spotter or chaperone, and I'd be the rigger. My job is to look after the ropes, and your pleasure. Lea's job is to ensure you're supported, and to assist me if I need." I grinned. "It's easier for two people to support a passed-out-from-pleasure person than one."

I found myself enjoying Frankie's flush, relishing her bold gaze as she offered me a flirty smile. "Alright, let me get on the mat."

She transitioned from her chair onto the floor, settling in the middle of the space, adjusting until her legs stretched out in front of her.

"Like this?"

I nodded, beginning to slowly circle her. "Perfect."

"What happens if there are only two of you?" She nodded toward Lea. "No chaperone?"

"You need to be extra careful. You use different ties, or supports like yoga bolsters or blocks. Everything is about the bunny and their experience."

Our gazes caught, held. In her eyes I read something I'd sorely missed—trust.

"What's next?" she asked, her voice catching.

"Level of sensuality or sexuality would be my next question. I might say, are you okay with kissing?"

Frankie hesitated, slowly nodding.

"What about sexual touching? For example, if I do a certain type of harness, I might need to move your breasts which I can achieve in a perfunctory manner, or I can touch you in a way that adds to your pleasure."

Her breath caught, a flush of arousal colouring her cheeks. "I-I'm good with sensual."

*Fuck.*

I nodded, my blood beginning to thicken.

"How about sensitive areas? Or areas where you have no feeling? Is there anything I should know about or look for?"

She ran a hand down her body, stopping a fraction above her abdomen. "I have limited feeling from here down, so any stimulation needs to be on the... rough side."

*Double fuck.*

I ignored the desire now burning in my gut. "Noted."

"And no movement or feeling in my upper thighs."

I made a mental note to use loose ties on her legs. "Any areas I should avoid?'"

She shook her head. "That's all."

"Because this is the first time we're working together, for this scene we'll keep your clothes on. If you want to change that next time, we'll renegotiate."

*Next time? What the fuck am I suggesting?*

We discussed safe words, and what aftercare might look like. Unable to stop myself, I stroked her cheek with the back of my hand, relishing the feel of her skin against mine.

*She's so fucking soft.*

"Any questions for me?"

Frankie shook her head, strands of her pink hair brushing across my fingertips.

"Are you ready?"

"Yes." Her breath caught as I shifted behind her, my body purposefully crowding hers. I reached around, holding my hands out in front of her, her body cradled by mine.

"Let's begin. Give me your hands."

Without hesitation she lifted her hands, settling them in mine. I slid the hair tie from her wrist, my hands running up her arms slowly then back down to grip her wrists, positioning her hands on either side of her for balance. Satisfied, I ran fingers through her hair, gathering her pastel pink locks in my hands.

She made a small sound as I gently massaged her scalp, encouraging her to relax under my touch.

"Okay?" I whispered, watching the small goose bumps prickle her skin.

"Yes."

To keep her hair free of the rope, I tied her locks in a bun, my hands slipping down her neck, across her shoulders and down her back, gliding over the material of her shirt, priming her body for the rope.

The warm spotlight painted shadows and highlights across Frankie's fair skin, and created a barrier between us and the rest of the class. I knew if I squinted, I'd see the faces of the watching class—but I wouldn't look. All my focus had to be on Frankie.

"Close your eyes, rainbow." The pet name felt right as it fell from my tongue.

If she'd noticed, Frankie didn't react. Her eyelids drifted slowly shut following my direction, a small exhale slipping free as she relaxed against my hands.

Tension pooled low in my gut, my cock aching at her submission.

"Good girl."

## 7

Frankie

My body bloomed under Jay's hands. I knew this was meant to be a class, I knew people were watching—but as he touched me it felt as if we were the only people in the room.

"Good girl."

My breath caught, my core clenching at the lazy drag of Jay's fingers across the curve of my neck. He leaned in, his breath tickling the shell of my ear sending tingles racing down my spine.

The weight of rope settled over my shoulders, Jay allowing the ends to slowly fall down my back.

"This," he said, his voice low. "Is the build up. Anticipation, uncertainty, pleasure—all are powerful drivers of desire."

Goose bumps pimpled my skin, the tiny hairs at the back of my neck lifting as his fingers dragged across my rib cage, the heat of them penetrating my thin shirt.

His knuckles grazed the curve of my breasts, his hands

stilling. Leaning close, he dropped his voice, his whisper meant for my ears only.

"No bra. Good girl."

I shuddered, Jay's name on the tip of my tongue.

*Hold it together, Frankie. This isn't sex. It's not even mutual attraction. It's... clinical. It's educational. It's—*

Jay slid one hand under my breasts, gently lifting them as rope settled around my rib cage.

"I'm going to tie a harness. It'll be snug but not tight."

I gasped as he let my breasts fall, the rope tightening around me.

"One finger," he said, voice rough. "Should be able to slip between the rope and the bunny's skin."

I expected him to demonstrate with a quick efficiency. But Jay—I was learning—wasn't one to rush. He slid a finger under the rope, his hand running slowly back and forth under my breasts, grazing the sensitive skin. I burned as his finger caught my shirt, dragging the soft fabric across my erect nipples.

I swallowed, biting the inside of my cheek to keep a moan from escaping.

*Clinical. He's just being a good guy and helping you to—*

Jay pressed a hand to my belly, my back plastering to his chest, rope falling around my middle.

"Oh," I breathed, my eyelids fluttering. "What are you—?"

"Eyes closed."

My lids slammed shut, my body instinctively obeying him.

*What kind of sexual sorcery is this? Surely I should be expressing some kind of moral outrage at how easily he's controlling me.*

But that was the thing about being a sexologist—I

accepted when I found something that got me off. And this rope-thing, it was hitting all my buttons.

Jay looped and knotted, petted and teased, binding me with both rope and touch. His hands wandered, his fingers a blunt taunt, building me until I could smell my arousal perfuming the air.

*Touch me. Please.*

Desperate to see if he felt even a fraction of my desire, my lids fluttered open, my gaze catching Jay's.

*Molten fire.*

His deep green eyes were ablaze with need, his expression fiercely intense.

My breath caught, a whimper escaping me.

"Sorry," I whispered, glancing down. "Oh."

His erection pressed against his zipper, his thick thighs flexing as he leaned in, his mouth a bare breath away from mine.

"Close. Your. Eyes."

I groaned, loud and needy, my lids squeezing shut.

"Jay...."

"We're going to bind your legs. Lea, can you help me?"

Uncertainty fluttered in my belly, my hands pressing into the mat.

"Jay." Breathy and threaded with dark desire, I didn't recognise my voice. "I'm not sure about this."

"It's your decision, Frankie."

I felt both of them hovering, waiting for me to decide what I wanted to do.

"Okay," I whispered, placing my faith in Jay. "Keep going."

He reached up, his rough hand cupping my cheek.

"I've got you, Frankie. Trust me."

## 8

**Jay**

I could smell her arousal, her body beginning to take on needy micro-movements—hips subtly rocking, her hands flexing, her back arching to offer her gloriously bound breasts.

*I need her naked and under me.*

I moved to Frankie's legs, Lea assisting me as I lightly bound them together. I'd long ago learned the power of stimulating the mind even as I played with a woman's body. The act of binding would be far more arousing than her being able to feel the ropes.

"Hands in front of you," I said, purposefully brushing my lips against her ear. Frankie shivered, her breath catching as she complied.

In deference to her seated position, I bound her hands in front of her ensuring that if she fell, she wouldn't crush her limbs. With practice and time, she'd learn to balance but for today I adjusted the harness for her needs.

*But next time, we might try something different.*

Desire warred with anticipation, my control pushed to the edge.

"Open your eyes."

She did, glancing down to see her bound torso and hands, but her gaze caught on her legs. I heard her small gasp, her body flowing like caramel against me as she relaxed into the restraint.

"Good girl," I praised, enjoying her slightly dazed expression. "Describe what you're feeling."

"Pressure," Frankie whispered, even that small noise loud in the silence of the room. "Tension. Heat, perhaps." She hesitated, her eyelids fluttering. "Freedom."

I guided Frankie to lay flat on the mat, my hands gliding over her skin as she let out little panting moans.

I took a mental picture, knowing I'd stroke my cock later to the memory of those needy little whimpers.

I let her lay bound for a few minutes allowing her to feel the ropes before shifting her, beginning to slowly unwind the binds.

My tone dropped, my praise for her ears only. "They loved seeing you, Frankie. They loved watching you."

She shivered in my arms, slumping against me as I finished freeing her.

"Aftercare," I explained, my voice intentionally low and soothing, my hands firm as I ran them over her arms, ensuring I touched every exposed inch of her glorious skin. "Is as essential as the negotiation."

Lea crouched beside me on the mat, her expression knowing as she placed a blanket over Frankie. Being mindful of Frankie's legs, we supported her, shifting her body until she was completely wrapped in the soft fabric.

Scene over, I turned to my silent students. "If you'd like to move to the cubicles, you'll find some rope and a printout of beginner ties. If you need anything, call. Lea and I will make our way around in a few minutes to check on you."

The class moved as one, hurrying toward the curtained stalls, eager to try what they had just witnessed.

"Norm," Mel said, sashaying her way across the room. "I'm gonna tie you tighter than a hog on Christmas."

"Looking forward to it, Melly-bear."

I exchanged an amused glance with Lea.

"You wanna check on them, or should I?" I asked, one hand resting on Frankie's shoulder, loathed to leave her.

"I'll do it." Lea rose to her feet, her latex suit making only the slightest sound. "Look after our girl." She tilted her head to one side, her expression thoughtful. "Do we need to talk about that scene?"

For the first time in a long time a small flush threatened to creep up my neck. "No."

She considered me slowly nodding. "Alright. But next time? Let me know before inviting audience participation. I would have worn something better suited to lifting people."

I accepted the quiet reprimand, following her a short distance away from Frankie to continue the conversation. "I didn't think she'd accept the invitation."

Lea cocked one eyebrow at me.

"But you're right," I conceded. "It won't happen again."

*It shouldn't have happened this time.*

Lea gave me a tight smile then moved to check on the class, leaving me with a shivering Frankie.

"You okay there, rainbow?" I asked, crouching beside her, unable to keep from running fingers through her soft hair.

"Frankie," she said softly, her eyes closed. "My name is Frankie. Rainbow is a stupid nickname."

I grinned. "But it suits you."

She opened her eyes enough to roll them at me, snapping them closed again, a smile tugging at one corner of her mouth. "That was quite the experience."

"Enough fodder for your podcast?"

She chuckled, slowly coming back to herself. "Maybe. We'll see."

"Well, any time you feel like another rope romp let me know. I'm always up for a scene."

"Bet you say that to all the girls."

*Not recently.*

And wasn't that a damned sad truth? The only time I'd set foot inside The A-List recently was to teach. Somewhere along the way my libido had taken a nosedive, my dick becoming as picky as a Southern Momma trying to find her virtuous daughter a husband.

"Help me up?" she asked, holding out a hand.

I helped her to sit upright, moving her wheelchair to her side, watching closely as she shifted until she could manoeuvre back into her chair.

"You don't need to watch," she said quietly, bending to settle her feet onto the foot rest.

"Actually, I do." I caught her hand twisting her arm to display the indentation left by the robes. My thumb stroked gently across her reddened skin. "A good rigger doesn't let you just walk out. We make sure you're okay. Our pleasure is bound up with yours, but your safety is always paramount."

Her breath caught, her cerulean eyes holding a shade of something I couldn't quite read.

"Jay, I—"

A loud moan interrupted her. We both looked to the cubicles, a soft chuckle escaping me when I recognised Norm's voice.

"Melissa! Fuck!"

"Is that—?"

I nodded, enjoying Frankie's startled giggle. "They do this every time."

"Melissa! Fuck. I think I'm in love!"

"You'd want to be after fifty years."

We smothered laughter, our gazes catching and holding as humour burned away leaving something much less innocent in its place.

"You feeling okay?" I asked, my voice gruff.

She nodded, her tongue flicking out to lick her lower lip.

*I want to taste her.*

"Jay, would you have dinner with me?"

I froze, blood pounding in my ears.

"What?"

"Dinner." She made an eating motion with her hands, her grin teasing. "Would you be interested?"

"As in a date?"

She nodded.

"I—" The words caught in my throat. "I don't date."

Frankie blinked. I saw disappointment and surprise then nothing, her thoughts shuttered.

"I'm sorry. I didn't—that is—" She stopped, sucking in a breath. "That's okay."

I caught her hand before she could escape. "But I'd love dinner."

We stared at each other, and for the first time since meeting, I couldn't read her.

Regret burned in my gut, a bitter taste on my tongue.

"Maybe another time," Frankie whispered, withdrawing her hand from mine. "I'll see you around, Jay."

I watched her move away from me, feeling as if the rainbow had melted away to leave a storm behind.

Lea moved to stand beside me, arms crossing over her chest.

"Fucked that one up," she commented, watching as the door shut behind Frankie.

"I don't do relationships."

And Frankie had commitment written all over her.

Lea snorted, rolling her eyes. "Yeah, sure. You keep telling yourself that." She clapped a hand on my shoulder. "Go check on the newbies, I've got a husband to get home to."

With a sigh and a final look toward the door, I moved to do as directed.

"And Jay?"

I glanced back at Lea.

"Next time a cute girl asks you out, accept the damn date."

## 9

Frankie

"You should call him," Annie said, licking the remains of yogurt from her spoon. "Or text. Either would work."

"Definitely," Mai agreed, forking a piece of tomato from her salad. "Offer to be friends. He seems like a good guy to know."

"You're all insane," I told them.

"Are we? Or are you chicken?" Flo asked, poking her tongue out at me.

I shut my mouth, viciously biting off a piece of my sandwich to keep from answering.

We were catching up at our weekly Wednesday lunch session. With the last dying weeks of summer still upon us, we'd decided to meet at the marina, settling in at one of the picnic tables lining the long boardwalk to enjoy the warmth of the sun.

Of course, Jay, and our experience at the kink club remained the hot topic of the day.

I swallowed, sighing loudly. "Can't we move on?"

"Absolutely not" Flo waved her hand in the air, her long fingers dancing. "You said, and I quote, 'It was the single most erotic experience of my life, and my clothes were on the whole time.'" She waggled a finger in my direction. "If that's not a sign you need to explore this further then I don't know what is."

I slumped, knocking my forehead against the table. "He's not that into me. Can't I give up? Why won't you bitches leave me alone."

Annie knuckled my head. "Because we love you. And while Mister-too-stupid-to-date-you is obviously not the one, he might know other guys who could be the answer to your spider removal woes."

"My what?" I asked, lifting my head.

"Frankie has spider issues?" Mai sent me a confused glance.

"Yes," Annie said solemnly, her expression serious. "In her vagina. There are cobwebs thick enough to—"

We all groaned, tossing lettuce leaves, napkins, and cutlery her way.

"So, are you going to call him?" Flo asked.

"I want to but I also don't want to." I sighed. "I mean the guy made it pretty fucking clear he's not interested."

"I can hear a but coming," Flo said in a sing-song voice.

"*But*," I said, emphasising the word. "You are all right. I wouldn't mind keeping him as a friend. He could be useful. And he did say that while he doesn't date he'd be open to dinner."

And—if I were honest with myself—I couldn't quite shake the idea of a fling with the hot rigger.

"So text the man." Annie shoved my cell at me. "Hurry! Now! Before you talk yourself out of it."

I took the cell, my fingers hovering over the screen.

*What do I even say?*

"Frankie, I swear, if you don't—"

"Hush!" I said to Mai, beginning to type. "I needed a moment to think."

Annie leaned over my shoulder, reading aloud as I hit send.

"Hi Jay, apologies for the late message, I've been busy."

"Simple but effective," Flo praised.

"I know you don't date so I thought I'd see if you'd like to have a platonic meal with me sometime. I've got a few more questions about accessible bondage I'd love to run past you ahead of next week's podcast. Thanks, Frankie." Annie gave my shoulder a squeeze. "Good job, babe. Short, sharp and to the point."

I tossed the cell on the table, slumping in my chair. "Why must men be difficult?"

"Because if they were easy, they'd be dogs."

I sputtered out a laugh, rolling my eyes at Annie. "You're a dope."

"And you're a stunning, beautiful woman who deserves every happiness." She wrapped me in a quick one-armed hug. "Don't let him get you down. Any man worth his salt would be lucky to—"

"He texted back!" Mai's hand shot into the air, my cell in her tight grasp.

"Oh, shit! What's it say?"

Mai handed it to me with a flourish. With trembling fingers, I unlocked the screen, reading his message aloud.

"Hey Frankie, great to hear from you. I'd love to catch up and chat some more. Would Friday night work for you? I also have something I'd like to discuss with you."

"And?" Flo prompted. "What else?"

"Nothing. Just that."

"Oh." Flo looked crestfallen but bounced back, her expression hopeful. "Well, it's positive he wants to have dinner with you."

"Oh, Flo." Mai wrapped an arm around her, pressing a kiss to her cheek. "You're such a romantic. Be honest, you're secretly hoping he'll fall in love with Frankie and they can play sexy cops and robbers for the rest of their days."

"It's crossed my mind once or twice."

I shook my head. "The chances of that happening are a million to one."

"But there's a chance."

"Not in this lifetime."

Flo ran hands through her hair, ruffling the strands until they fell in an auburn wave over her breast.

"And yet," she said slowly, her expression thoughtful. "You're still going to go to dinner with a little hope in your heart. Who's the romantic now?"

"It better *not* be you." Annie pointed her spoon at me. "You're only meeting him to get the hook up on actual date-able guys who like to do naughty things in the bedroom. And their friends—please find dates for us all. All our vaginas are in need of fun times."

My cell rang, the ringtone the one I used exclusively for clients.

"Shit, I've got to take this." I snatched my sandwich, dumping it in my lap as I wheeled back from the table. "I'll see you guys next week."

"Text us about the date," Mai ordered. "We want all the details."

"And be open to the possibility of the what if," Flo yelled after me. "What if he does kiss you? Think about it!"

I rolled my eyes, moving away from the table to take the call.

"Lucy, how are you?"

"Oh, Frankie, you'll never guess what happened. I let Leanne kiss me."

As I started back to my office, listening to my client gush about her breakthrough, I found my thoughts wandering to Jay.

*What if he does kiss you?*

My traitorous body gave a little shimmer.

*What if indeed.*

## 10

**Jay**

"I told you, it's not a fucking date."

"Uh-huh." Ren twirled the basketball on a finger, his knowing expression pissing me off.

"I mean it."

"I'm sure you do." He caught the ball, tossing it to me. "And where are you going to dinner again?"

I caught the pass, bouncing it on the worn floor of the rec centre before tossing it back, refusing to answer his question.

I'd made the mistake of telling Ren about Frankie and now our weekly basketball game seemed in jeopardy of being converted from competition to gossip-fest.

*Note to self, don't ever tell Ren another thing.*

"Oh, that's right. The Bronze Horseman, isn't it?" He grinned, throwing me another pass. "But it's definitely *not* a date."

The Bronze Horseman had garnered a reputation as the

place where desperate-to-couple-up-singles took dates in a last-ditch attempt to seal the deal.

"Doesn't matter where," I said, tossing the ball from hand to hand. "The main thing is that Frankie knows this isn't a date."

"Mmhmm. And yet you thought to mention this non-date to me." Ren caught my slightly too-hard pass with a little huffing laugh. "Doth, thou protest too much?"

"Fuck you."

"Nah, you're not my type." He tossed the ball back to me with a laugh.

"You boys gonna chat all day or we gonna play?" Linc asked, strolling onto the court stride for stride with his twin, Theodore—though God forbid if anyone called him anything but Theo.

"Fuck no" I moved to the centre of the court. "Let's play."

The four of us fell into two teams, the brothers on opposing sides. Ren and I were tall and lean, adding speed to our respective duo. The brothers were all bulk—muscles upon muscles—their bodies built for the offensive backfield, not the basketball court. We played first to seventy points, the losers having to buy the first round of drinks at the bar later. Occasionally those rounds included an order of ice for bruises.

With only one point to go, I passed to Theo who charged at his brother, shifting to one side at the last moment. Anticipating his move, Linc mirrored him, both going down in a tumble of limbs, Theo landing on the bottom.

"Ah fuck!"

"Shit!"

Ren and I jogged over, crouching beside the brothers.

"Damn. Sorry, bro." Linc pushed to a stand, holding out his hand. "Prosthetic okay?"

Theo nodded, accepting his brother's hand. "That's a foul, you motherfucker."

Linc grinned, bumping his shoulder. "I believe you fouled me, dickhead."

"They're fine." Ren rolled his eyes. "Let's finish this."

"You sure," I asked, collecting the ball and tossing it at Linc. "You don't want to retire injured?"

"Fuck you. Get on the court."

I grinned, shooting Theo an eyebrow wiggle. "I believe that gives us the advantage."

"That double shot of top-shelf whiskey is gonna taste real nice."

It was a hard-fought battle, but Theo managed to slip one past Ren, the ball finding the hoop.

"Score!" I slapped palms with Theo, shooting finger guns at our opposition. "I'll take a triple scotch, thanks, boys."

"Over my dead body. You're both getting a jug of tap beer and you'll be fucking happy with it," Linc ordered, hands on his knees as he sucked in air.

"Winners pick."

We made our way to the locker rooms, tossing insults and rehashing the finer points of the game.

"Speaking of winners." Ren sent me a sly smile. "Has Jay told you about his date-not-date with Frankie Kenton?"

I shot him a glare. "You wanna shut your gossip hole?"

"You? On a date?" Linc asked, eyebrows raising. "Bullshit."

"Did the world end? Are pigs flying?" Theo lifted a hand to his forehead pretending to peer up at the sky.

"Fuck all of you. Seriously. Just for that, I'm gonna order the whole fucking bottle of Hennessy."

My cell dinged with an incoming text.

"Could it be the woman of the hour?" Ren asked, trying to grab the cell from my hand.

"Fuck you!" I shoved his face away with one hand, turning my back on my so-called friends. "You guys are the worst."

"And you're too easy to rile."

I looked down at the text, ignoring the little frisson of anticipation when Frankie's name appeared on the screen.

> **FRANKIE**
>
> Bronze Horseman works for me but only if you buy dessert. I expect the triple cherry pie or I'm out.

I tapped out a quick reply, ignoring the kissing sounds coming from behind me.

> **JAY**
>
> Cherry pie? Rainbow, I'm not sure we can be friends. The chocolate lover is where it's at. Brownie, chocolate mousse, chocolate gelato, and a side of chocolate sauce? It's the only option.

> **FRANKIE**
>
> We'll have to agree to disagree. Which is fine because it means I get dessert to myself.

I chuckled, sliding the cell into my pocket.

"See what I mean?" Ren asked, sending Linc and Theo an amused grin. "The boy has it bad."

I flicked him the bird. "Get your asses showered, I need a drink."

Later that night I opened Frankie's Instagram finding a new photo. She had a length of rope in one hand and a saucy smile on her cherry-red lips. The caption read,

*Think it's (k)not for you? Wait until you hear all about accessible bondage.*

My hand slid down my body, fisting my cock. Memories of Frankie's responsiveness hit me, her needy moans burned into my brain.

"Fuck it." I tossed my cell away, closing my eyes as I stroked my dick, desperate to know if the woman who looked like a rainbow would taste of sugar or spice.

As I spilled into my hand, one thought solidified.

*I need to taste her.*

**Jay**

I hovered outside The Bronze Horseman, fiddling with my tie and questioning, for the millionth time, why I'd bothered to wear a suit to a non-date.

"I look like a fucking chump."

"I don't know, I think you look quite nice."

I jerked back, looking over my shoulder to find Frankie heading toward me, her smile wide.

*Oh, shit.*

She looked like a wet dream—pink hair twisted into some kind of complicated but sexy topknot, the loose strands floating around her face made my fingers itch with the need to brush them back. Her lips were painted a hot pink, her eyes smokey. She wore a low-cut white top, a leather jacket, and knee-high black boots. My gaze caught on her dark wash jeggings, and I fought a sudden urge to peel them from her body.

*Fuck.*

"Shit. I didn't see you there. Sorry, I—"

She stopped in front of me, tipping her head to one side, a small grin playing on her delicious lips. "Jay?"

"Yeah?"

"Are you nervous?"

I stuttered out a laugh. "No. Well, maybe. It's been a while since I've been out to dinner with just a friend."

Frankie's brows arched, her grin turning teasing. "And if I weren't 'just a friend,' would you still be wearing a suit and tie?"

"That depends on if there are benefits involved."

Frankie laughed, her grin wide and genuine. "Unfortunately for you, there are few benefits to being friends with me. I mostly end up psychoanalysing and prying into your sex life."

"Sounds like my kind of friend. Shall we?" I asked, gesturing at the door.

"Sure."

I held it open for her with a flourish, enjoying her amusement at my antics.

"Right this way," the hostess said, leading us through the restaurant. "We've got you at one of our private tables tonight."

Frankie sent me a look over her shoulder.

"What?"

"You ordered a private table?"

I shrugged. "No biggie. Just assumed you wouldn't want our conversation overheard."

"Uh-huh."

"What's that supposed to mean?"

She gave me an innocent shrug. "Nothing."

Decked out in bronze, wood, and concrete, The Bronze Horseman had to be the classiest but most welcoming restaurant in Capricorn Cove. The owners had worked hard to make the place fancy without being pretentious—a tough act to pull off.

I reached out, gliding my hand along a wooden wall panel, enjoying the feel of it under my palm. I used it to centre myself because—if I were man enough to admit it, and I was—Frankie had thrown me.

"Here we are, best table in the house."

I shrugged out of my jacket taking a seat, Frankie scooting into the space across from me.

"Can I start you with some drinks?" the hostess asked, handing us menus.

Frankie shot me a grin. "I'm ready to order if you are?"

"Two meat-lover burgers?" I asked, referring to our text conversation throughout the week.

She nodded. "And cherry pie for dessert."

"Ah, no, I believe we agreed on the chocolate lover."

"We certainly did not."

The hostess chuckled. "How about one of each?"

"If you insist," Frankie said with a dramatic sigh. "And two of your house ciders."

"Great, I'll be back shortly."

We handed our menus to the hostess and settled in, staring at each other from across the table.

"It seems this is becoming a habit."

"What is?"

"Staring awkwardly at each other."

I snorted, lifting the water carafe to pour us both a glass. "Is it a kink I should know of?"

A startled laugh escaped her. "Wow. You dive right in there."

"What's the point of small talk? Let's get deep."

"Innuendo, Jay!"

I chuckled, appreciating her quick wit.

"Let me review what I know about you. You're a master at foreplay but terrible at small talk." She pretended to write on the palm of her hand. "And when did you realise you had commitment issues?"

I groaned. "So this is the judgment men have to look forward to on dates with you?"

"Uh-huh." She waggled a finger at me. "Not a date, remember?"

"Mm."

A harried-looking waiter arrived, setting down our drinks before quickly scurrying back to the bar.

"What shall we toast to?" Frankie asked, lifting her glass.

"World peace?"

She made a dismissive sound. "While people have free will that ain't happening, my friend. Pick something more realistic."

"How about to us? To a long and beautiful friendship."

"I'll agree with that."

We clinked glasses, taking a long drink.

"Alright," Frankie said, licking foam from her lip. "Tell me all about you. I want to know everything."

"Not much to know. Single, work with my dad at his lumber yard. Though, I guess it's mine too, since I bought into it a few years back. We own forest plantations around the country and have been working to make them as sustainable and eco-friendly as possible."

"Is that even possible with forestry?"

I nodded. "We're working with scientists to explore better ways of doing things. For example, only growing certain types of trees in local areas. It's why we have a few farms in other states."

"That's cool. Do you enjoy it?"

I took a sip of the cider. "Not as much as the carpentry

side. I enjoy creating things."

"Any examples I'd know of?"

I gestured at the restaurant. "All the wood details are mine."

She glanced around, her smile approving. "This is beautiful. You're really talented."

I brushed off her praise. "Your turn. Don't keep a guy waiting, why the podcast?"

She shrugged. "*All Access* was a whim. I had a client who'd experienced a temporary physical ailment. The information they'd found online didn't give them any information about what was okay to engage in sex-wise. I went home, rang my friends and asked them to tell me about the weirdest sex or body-related thing they'd ever tried to Google. Most of it was sex stuff and the information had been surprisingly lacking. Over a bottle of wine, a laptop, and a teleconference, *All Access* was born."

"So, it's about sex?" I asked, making a mental note to add some episodes to my playlist.

"God no. It's about anything to do with accessibility. Sure, we talk about sex because—hello, I'm a sexologist—but I also invite guests on to talk about different topics like mental health, the importance of movement, shame—you name it, we talk about it. This is a podcast that doesn't have any closed doors."

"Ah, hence the name."

Frankie beamed. "You got it."

Clever, witty, and with an enthusiasm that sparked my own, Frankie was the kind of woman who I referred to as a sun. She sucked people into her orbit, bathing them in her glow.

If I wasn't careful, one of us could get burned.

Badly.

## 12

___

Frankie

I nursed a cup of coffee, laughing at Jay's disgruntled expression as he tried a piece of my pie.

"Good?" I asked, giggling at his disgust.

"No. Desserts shouldn't involve fruit."

I snorted, rolling my eyes. "And what is that?" I pointed at his chocolate-dipped strawberry.

"Well, it can involve fruit but only if there's chocolate involved." He absently pushed his sleeve back to his bicep, simultaneously revealing his tattoos and making him eleventy-billion times hotter.

*Friends. Mutual acquaintances. Put him in the friend bubble, Frankie. The guy doesn't belong anywhere near your heart's end zone.*

"Alright, I need to know. What's with the Lego tattoos?" I asked, nodding at the impressive ink on his right arm.

"Childhood memories." His flat tone sent some red flags flying.

"Good ones, I hope?"

He tapped one of the minifig images on his arm. "This one is."

I cocked an eyebrow. He caught my look, sending me an eye roll.

"Don't psychoanalyse me, Frankie. It's rather unbecoming."

I chuckled but didn't like the defensive wall he'd thrown up between us.

He watched me sip my coffee.

"Fine." He sighed. "I'll give in. The first toy that was ever just mine was a box of Lego. An X-wing."

"How old were you?"

"Twelve."

I blinked. "Twelve? That's the first time you owned a toy?"

He cupped his mug of coffee. "The first toy that wasn't some other kids first."

I'd heard something like this from previous clients.

"Foster care?"

Jay nodded. "In and out of group homes and distant relatives' places before they got sick of taking me in."

"That must have been hard."

He shrugged. "They were all just waiting rooms." He paused, the silence stretching as he stared into his coffee.

"Waiting rooms for?" I prompted gently.

"My mother to sober up."

I winced. "I'm sorry. Addiction sucks."

Jay shrugged, shifting in his chair. "Shit happens. I think I read somewhere one in five people are dealing with some form of addiction. I'm nothing special."

I itched to reject his statement. "And no one gave you a toy?"

"Sure, they did. But used ones that were missing eyes or

arms or borrowed toys I had to leave behind because there was always some other kid who'd need something to play with after I left."

My heart began to ache, my chest tight. "Damn."

Jay shrugged. "It is what it is. Can't change the past." He ran a hand through his hair. "Fuck, this all sounds sadder than it was. I'm not some broken kid looking for love."

I let his statement pass without comment.

"Do you still keep in contact with your mom?"

He shook his head. "She's been sober for about six years but we're not close."

"That's good for her but I'm sorry you don't have a relationship."

"Yeah." He looked down at his coffee. "Shit happens."

I cleared my throat. "And the Lego?" I asked, circling back to the happier memory.

"Will." Jay smiled, his twinkle returning. "First week I lived with the fucker, he took me shopping with the rest of his boys. Walked us into the mall and said, 'Here's a fifty. Go get yourself something nice.'"

I grinned, leaning forward. "I'm surprised you didn't run."

He laughed. "Thought about it for about five seconds but decided I really, *really* wanted to spend it on myself."

"And you bought the X-wing?"

He nodded, letting out a dreamy sigh. "Came with a complete set of minifigs." He tapped the tattoos on his bicep. "Started my love of Lego."

"You seem like the kind of guy to still have a bunch lying around the house."

"A bunch? Frankie, I have a Lego room."

I laughed, delighted. "I love that you play."

It was his turn to cock an eyebrow.

"Not like that!" I threw my wadded-up napkin at him. "Well, maybe like that. But I mean joyful play."

"Oh, I know exactly what joyful play is." He wiggled his eyebrows suggestively. "I'm pretty sure I heard it from you last—"

"I'm serious!" I interrupted him, blushing furiously. "Adults forget to fuel their inner child. And those who had childhood experiences taken away—the kids who grew up far too fast—they deserve it more than most. Play is, and should always be considered, a birthright. Just as breathing, and living, and existing in happiness should be a birthright." I reached across the table, tangling my fingers with his. "I'm really glad you're nourishing your inner child."

"Well, shit." He huffed out a laugh, his fingers clenching around mine. "Here I was thinking a grown man playing with toys is pretty sad."

"Never." I gave his hand one final squeeze, then sat back, lifting my coffee cup to my lips, giving him a teasing wink. "Besides, we all like toys."

"And what toys do you happen to have, Ms. Frankie?" His grin was pure mischief.

I'm not sure what it was, but I decided to tease him a little. I lifted one shoulder in a half-shrug. "If this were a date, I might have invited you back to look in my toy drawer."

Jay fell back in his seat, his hands pressed to his chest.

"Jesus! Low blow, Frankie."

I smirked over the rim of my mug. "You walked right into that one."

"I did. And I'm regretting my no-date policy."

"About that." I leaned in, tipping my head to one side. "Why don't you date? Or is that just a thing you say to women you're not interested in?"

"I'd just like the record to show I am extremely interested in you and if you'd given me even a hint you were the kind of woman open to a friends-with-benefits situation then this would be a very different date."

"How do you know I'm not?" I asked, insulted by his assumption.

He grinned. "Am I wrong?"

I rolled my eyes, admitting the truth. "No, and I hate that you knew it."

"Frankie?"

I turned, finding Christine hovering near our table.

"Oh, hey! I didn't know you were coming here tonight."

She shot me a grin. "Date night." She turned to Jay, giving him an approving once-over. "And hello, Frankie's date." She thrust her hand at him. "I'm Christine, her producer."

"Jay." He shook her hand. "Though this isn't a date."

"More like a work meeting," I clarified.

"For the podcast? Oh!" She snapped her fingers. "You're the kink guy."

Jay chuckled. "Rigger. But yes, that's me."

Chrissy raised a finger to her chin, considering him. "Jay, can you say 'She sells sea shells by the seashore' for me?"

Jay sent me a questioning look which I returned with a shrug.

"Sure. She sells sea shells by the sea shore."

"Subject to Frankie's thoughts, how would you like to guest star on our show next week?"

"Wait," I said, my gaze snapping to Christine. "What?"

"He's got the voice for it, Frankie. And the skills. You can talk about the experience and he can talk about the practice." She mouthed the word *Poddie* at me.

I stared at her for a beat then swung to look at Jay. "Well, shit. She's not wrong. You in?"

He shrugged, a devilish smile on his lips. "Depends, will I get a peek at your toys?"

My face flamed, heat burning my cheeks.

"Toys?" Chrissy asked. "Oh, you mean her figurine collection?"

I pressed my lips together to keep nervous giggles from spilling over.

"Something like that," Jay murmured, his green gaze still locked with mine.

"Will you do it?" I asked, my mirth finally under control. "Please?"

He hesitated. "Sure."

Christine squealed, pulling Jay's attention from me, gushing to give him all the details while I watched, sipping my coffee.

*This is a bad idea.*

I knew it, and yet, right now I couldn't seem to care.

"Wonderful. We'll see you on Wednesday, Jay."

"Can't wait."

Jay turned back to me as Chrissy walked away. I caught her look over his head, rolling my eyes as she pointed at him mouthing *Oh my God* behind his back and shooting me a thumbs-up.

"You cool with this?" Jay watched me, his gaze searching.

"Of course. Why do you ask?"

He shrugged. "The podcast is your baby. I don't want to encroach on your safe space."

A rush of warm gooey feelings had me linking our fingers once again. "Safe spaces are great but brave spaces are where it's at for me. And brave spaces mean inviting people in and building connections that might not other-wise exist. They're all about constructive discomfort."

His fingers flinched, but his hand remained in mine.

"You're a good woman, Frankie Kenton."

I beamed at him releasing his hand, determined not to push my luck.

Jay gestured at my empty coffee cup. "You finished?"

I nodded.

"Can I walk you to your car?"

"I'd love that."

We paid, having a brief tussle over the bill.

"You can pay next time."

"Fine," I sighed. "But that means you're eating fruit-laden dessert."

"Over my dead body."

Jay shoved open the heavy door, holding it as I wheeled through, his expression pensive as he looked up at the sky. "Clear night."

"Mm."

The stars twinkled above us, the air cool.

"I'm gonna miss this temperature in the next few months. Working with wood in the cold is a fucking bitch. If only summer lasted forever. "

I sent a bittersweet smile Jay's way. "You would say that."

His eyebrows lifted. "Let me guess, you're a winter child?"

"Of course." I tapped my chair. "As much as I love Pinkie, she doesn't come with AC. Someone should get on that."

"Pinkie?"

I nodded, grinning up at him as we wandered down the sidewalk toward my car. "She's Pinkie, I'm the brain. Get it?"

"I like it. Do you own just the one?"

"No, I actually have three. Pinkie's my every day but I

have an all-terrain so I can go to the beach and on hikes and so on. I also have a chair for home use."

"Interesting. I'd never really thought about—wait." He laughed, stopping on the sidewalk. "Is this your car?"

I turned my chair slightly toward him, cocking an eyebrow. "Are you disparaging Dolly Parton?"

He shook his head. "I should have known. I really should have known."

My pink Jetta sat shining in the moonlight.

"What did you expect?"

Jay shrugged. "I don't know. A minivan maybe?"

I crossed my arms over my chest. "Really?"

"I guess I assumed you'd roll into the car."

"Ah, I see."

He narrowed his gaze on me. "What was that tone?"

I patted his jacketed arm. "It's okay. I forgive you for being ignorant."

He snorted. "No, you don't."

"No, I really don't." I gestured at Dolly. "She's specifically built for me to drive. I transition using a slide board, and drive using hand controls."

Jay nodded, his expression thoughtful. "Is it easy?"

I snorted, rolling toward Dolly. "Rethink your question."

He had the grace to blush.

"You want to watch, don't you?"

"Actually, I want to check out the hand controls." He sent me a wink. "But I'm always open to watching."

I rolled my eyes, fighting a blush. "Typical man-child. Let me guess, you're imagining my steering wheel as a game controller."

He nodded, a teasing glint in his eyes.

"Spoiler—they're not. Come on."

I pulled open my door, sliding out my board and quickly

transitioning into the car. Once in the driver's seat, I adjusted my legs then broke down my chair, hauling it in to sit it in the passenger seat.

"Impressive."

"What? Getting into a car? Yes, you're right. That was an absolute triumph of the human spirit."

Jay chuckled. "I'm doing it again, aren't I?"

"Yep."

"Sorry. I'll try to be less ableist."

"I'd appreciate the effort."

He gestured at the controls. "Would it be too much to ask if I could get a ride home? I'm keen to see it in action."

"You're weird, but because you paid for dessert, I'll forgive you." I jerked a thumb at the passenger seat. "Move Pinkie back and I'll give you a ride."

## 13

**Jay**

"Alright." I settled in the car, slapping my hands on my knees. "Let's go, speed racer! Show me what this baby can do."

Frankie laughed, switching the ignition on. "We'll be doing the speed limit, thank you very much. You may have money to waste on bail, but the colour orange has never looked good on me."

"You're no fun. Vin Diesel would be very disappointed."

I enjoyed her snort as she began to reverse, her hands moving on the levers on either side of her steering wheel.

"Where do you live?" she asked, the car idling at the entrance to The Bronze Horseman parking lot.

"I'm down on Elm. Near the rec centre. You'll know my house when you see it."

"That statement scares me on multiple levels." She flicked the indicator, pausing before turning onto the near-empty road, following the boardwalk. With no other traffic, we had a clear view of the moon dancing on the ocean.

"Sometimes I think about leaving the Cove," Frankie said quietly. "But then I go for drives on nights like tonight and am reminded of how spectacular living here is. It's as if nature's purposefully demonstrating how beautiful the world is."

"I know what you mean. I used to think it'd be the worst thing in the world to stay."

"And yet here you are." She gave me a meaningful look.

I ran a hand through my hair. "I left after the affair with the cougar. Travelled around the world for two years, back-packing through Europe, South America, Australia."

"Didn't find what you were looking for?"

*I doubt I ever will.*

"Nope. And it surprised me how much I missed the family. Ended up back here despite my best efforts."

Frankie turned onto my street and for a second I consid-ered telling her I'd moved, fighting a near-overwhelming need to prolong my time with her.

*What the fuck is wrong with me?*

"Third on the left."

As we pulled up, I waited for her reaction—delighted when she didn't disappoint. Stunned amusement, a growing smile, pure joy in her big blue eyes.

"I should have guessed," she said, parking the car. "Of course, this is your house. Of course, it is."

The small bungalow wasn't much to look at inside or out. I'd been slowly fixing her up over the last few months but still had a long way to go. I'd purchased her from a widower who'd decided to move closer to his grandkids. The roof had been a complete redo, the entire frame sagging and waterlogged from years of neglect.

My family had given me shit about the sale, begging me

to reconsider. But I'd signed on the dotted line—all because of the yard. The glorious, jungle of a yard.

"I—I'm not even sure where to start."

"Well, let's see." I pointed to the brachiosaurus. "That's Bob. He likes leaves, slippery slides, and not being eaten by Chad."

"And Chad would be?"

I pointed at the T-rex hiding amongst the willow trees.

"Ah." Frankie nodded solemnly, her eyes dancing. "Of course."

"Then you have Martha, Arthur, and Harold."

"Let me guess, the raptors?"

I beamed at her. "Got it in one."

She gestured at the triceratops family clustered in the middle of the yard. "And those are?"

"Triceratops."

She cocked an eyebrow. "What, no names?"

I shook my head. "Of course not, Frankie. They're triceratops. You don't *name* them."

She burst out laughing, her head tipping back as her delight spilled free.

My control snapped. I leaned across the console, cupping her cheek to turn her face to me.

Her laughter stuttered, her eyes widening.

"Just so we're clear," I murmured gruffly. "This doesn't mean we're on a date."

"W-w-what?"

I kissed her, and to my fucking horror found she didn't taste like sugar *or* spice.

She tasted like forever.

## 14

**Frankie**

*This can't be happening.*

Jay pressed a hot kiss to my mouth, his short beard grazing my cheeks. His tongue stroked the seam of my mouth with sensual ease, my lips parting to grant him entrance.

My mind couldn't comprehend this reality. One second we were talking about dinosaurs, the next Jay's tongue was in my mouth doing things I didn't even know a tongue could do.

Shock held me rigid, my body tense. Then he made a sound—the noise so raw, so needy, so utterly male, I melted like an ice cream on a summer's day.

*What a tongue. What a beard. What a fucking delight.*

He took advantage of my surprise, claiming my mouth with possessive demand. My traitorous nipples began to tingle, a deep ache building inside me.

I leaned into his kiss, my tongue tangling with his, my hands fisting his suit jacket, desperate for more.

*So much for the friend zone.*

The fact Jay kept denying our connection was a big fuck off red flag. If this were Annie, Flo, or Mai I'd be advising them to tuck, duck, and roll the fuck out of this situation.

So why was I protesting as Jay pulled back? Why did my fingers tangle in his tie? Why did I yank him to me? Why did I moan when our mouths collided?

"Frankie."

My name on Jay's lips snapped me out of it.

"Fuck." I let his tie slip from between my clenched fist.

"You can say that again."

My lipstick smudged his mouth and I found I liked the look of it there, liked knowing I'd left my mark on him.

My gaze dropped to his lap, pleased to find him as turned on as me.

"You're going to be trouble, Doctor Kenton."

With regret I lifted my gaze, attempting to shove all my emotions into a box. "We shouldn't have done that. You shouldn't have done that."

"No," he agreed, scrubbing a hand over his face, his palm rasping against his short beard. "I'm sorry."

"Why did you?"

Our gazes met and held in the dark cabin of the car, a million words and emotions passing unspoken between us, none of which made any sense.

"Because I couldn't stop myself. You're making me break all my rules, Frankie. And it's fucking annoying."

Despite myself, pleasure unfurled, warming at his frustrated admission.

"We're still not dating, right?"

"Right." He huffed out a laugh. "You're the kind of woman who should come with a warning label."

"What? Loves trashy reality TV shows and fails at cooking?"

"Makes a man lose his goddamn mind."

I stared at him. "Jay, you should get out of the car before I start kissing you again."

"I know." He didn't move.

"Jay... please. Go."

"Fuck it." He shifted, his gaze penetrating. "Frankie, let me friendship date you. Let me frate you."

I stared at him. "What?"

"I'm a shitty boyfriend, I'm terrible in relationships. But damn if I don't want to try with you."

I put aside the first half of his statement to dissect later. "And by friendship date you mean..?"

"Work out if we're compatible? Dress up. Fuck, I don't know." He ran a hand through his hair. "What do people do on dates?"

I tried not to giggle at his melodramatic woe-is-me expression.

"Basically what we did tonight. Only there's normally kissing involved." I crossed my arms over my chest, attempting to ignore the press of my nipples against the cups of my bra. "You're gonna have to explain to me how friendship dating is different to romantic dating. Or... you know. Friendship."

"Frating," he corrected with a lopsided grin. "And the first rule of frating is no sex."

I spluttered. "What? No sex?"

"You heard me. Sex gets in the way."

I stared at him. "Sex gets in the—"

"Stop repeating me." He caught my hand, giving it a squeeze. "You're making it weird. I'm attempting to be gallant here."

"Withholding the D from a relationship is a violation of at least four Human Rights."

He chuckled but quickly sobered. "Please, babe. I'm trying here."

I considered him for a long moment, struggling with the weight of this decision.

I wasn't the kind of girl who indulged in a fling. Power to everyone who relished those experiences but I wasn't built that way. I needed the back-and-forth, the give-and-take. I needed the safety and certainty that came with being in a relationship. And getting involved with Jay felt anything but certain.

I also needed sex. I loved sex, I loved being embraced and petted, I loved touch and feel. If I were to identify my love languages, physical touch would be right up there.

But even knowing my heart might get broken, even deciding he had terrible fucking idea written all over him, even with the obvious red flags, I couldn't seem to stop myself.

"What are we talking? Kissing?" I asked. "Is kissing allowed?"

He hesitated. "Do friends kiss?"

"Some do," I lied.

"Then yes."

"What about holding hands?"

"Sure."

"And—"

"Frankie!" Jay snapped, a muscle jumping in his jaw. "Yes or no?"

"I'm still deciding. This seems like a big deal for you."

His lips quirked. "It is. I've never tried this with anyone else."

I nodded. "So what you're proposing is something like friends-with-benefits but without the benefits?"

He grinned. "We can do benefits, just above the belt."

"This seems like a terrible idea."

He sighed, scrubbing hands over his face. "I like you, Frankie. You intrigue me. But it's been a long fucking time since I've been anything but a notch on someone's bed post." He caught one of my hands in both of his. "You're not—"

"If you finish that sentence with, 'like other girls' this relationship is over before it even begins."

He laughed. "I was going to say my normal type." His hands squeezed mine. "This is a big step outside my comfort zone."

I sucked in a breath deciding to follow my gut and take a chance. "If this is what you need then I'll try."

"Fuck yes."

I hid a smile. "But only if you promise me one thing."

He cocked one eyebrow.

"Bring your ropes to the recording on Wednesday."

His face shuttered. "I thought you were cool with no sex. That includes kink."

"You'll have to break the no kink rule for this week. I need images of the different ties for my listeners."

"Really?"

"Yes."

"You won't try to seduce me?"

"Oh, I'll be tempted to try." I admitted. "But I'll also be respectful of what you're asking. Relationships are a two-way street, Jay. I won't ask you to break boundaries as long as you're willing to communicate your needs and respect and answer mine."

"And what are your needs?"

I licked my lips, stunned we were jumping into this shit so quickly.

*But since he's been honest with me, I better lay it all out.*

"I need praise and touch. I need you to be there when I call. I need a friend as much as I need a lover—more so. Love, eros, that lusty feeling, it all eventually disappears. But companionship, true connection—that's what's important." I sucked in a breath. "And I need you to wash your hands before you touch my vulva."

He blinked. "Jesus. How did we get to genitals?"

"We're talking about needs here. And while we're not discussing sex, it might happen so I need you to know exactly what sex looks like for me."

He licked his lips. "Okay, shoot."

"If I get a UTI I can end up in hospital. So I need your hands to be clean. I need to pee after sex, and I need to wash up after as well. Same goes for oral. It's not sexy, but it keeps me healthy."

Jay nodded, expression thoughtful.

I sucked in a breath. "I sometimes need lube, I sometimes don't. It's better to be prepared so I like to always have some available."

"I'll add lube to the shopping list."

I grinned. "But no sex, right?"

He nodded, his expression sobering. "But I'm man enough to admit you tempt the hell out of me."

"I appreciate your honesty and that's flattering."

We grinned at each other.

"Anything else I should know?"

"Final thing, the G-spot is best for orgasms but I can feel strong stimulation almost everywhere when you're playing with me. My clit is particularly sensitive but my nerves are shot. Rough movements are wonderful, but sometimes my nerves start misfiring and I interpret that as an attack or pain. It's confusing as fuck and means I have to stop and recalibrate." I searched his face for any sign of discomfort. "Okay," I gave him a lopsided smile. "I'm opening the floor to questions."

He snorted, reaching out to entwine our fingers. "You do know no sex means no sex, right?"

I nodded.

"But I appreciate you giving me the heads up. Nothing you've said scares me, Frankie. Everything is a part of who you are—and who you are is someone I want to know more. Frating might sound like a terrible idea but sex is... complicated. I want more for us. I haven't had a true relationship in a long time. I joke about not knowing how to date and it's slightly true. I haven't dated for companionship in a long time. Sex? Yes. Friendship?" He shook his head. "I don't know what's going to happen between us, but I know I want you in my life."

The warm gooey feeling returned with a vengeance.

"We'll go as slow as you need." I pulled back, booping him on the nose with one finger. "Except for the ropes. I actually do need you to tie me up for my job."

His slow grin put me in mind of sultry nights and lazy mornings. He leaned across the console cupping my check to press a final chaste kiss to my still sensitive lips.

"I'll bring the ropes." He leaned his forehead against mine, his green gaze piercing. "Good night, friend."

His fingers dragged softly across my skin before he reached behind him to open the door and stepped free from the car. He moved quickly, shifting my chair back to the passenger seat and gently shut the door. I expected him to head inside but he crouched slightly, his hands raised in the shape of a rectangle.

"What are you doing?"

"Taking a mental picture." He pretended to click, acting as if he held a camera. "Straight to the spank bank."

I groaned, flicking him the finger. "Good night, Jay Wood."

"Good night, Frankie Kenton."

I watched him walk backwards, still snapping pretend pictures of me.

*Did I really want to friend-date this guy?*

Jay tripped backward into one of the dinosaurs, arms flailing wildly to keep from toppling over. He righted, patting the statue, sending me a large grin and a thumbs-up.

That warm sensation settled in my gut—a feeling I'd begun associating with Jay.

*Well, fuck. Yes. Yes, I did.*

## 15

Frankie

"What time is he coming over?"

I glanced at the clock at the bottom of my laptop screen. "In about an hour, why?"

Annie shook her head, her wild hair filling the entire square of my screen. "I cannot believe you're even contemplating this. He wants to—what did you call it?"

"Frate."

"Being an idiot is what I call it. No sex? Babe, you're gonna get your heart broken."

Annie had called this emergency videoconference after I'd messaged them about the non-date. It seemed she was concerned for my soul—a surprising shift from her previous concern for my vagina.

"I disagree," Mai interrupted, moving this way and that on the small screen as she massaged dye into cloth, the camera following her movement. "He's a nice guy. He's friends with Ren and, sure, he hasn't had the best track record with girlfriends—"

Annie snorted.

"—but, his willingness to try is a good sign."

I pinched the bridge of my nose. "Looks like we've got a one-one split. Flo, you're the deciding vote."

"You know my thoughts."

"Flo's biased!" Annie protested. "She's swayed by unrealistic expectations of men. I blame romance novels."

"It's not unrealistic to expect a guy to sweep me off my feet. Life imitates art all the time, and don't we all deserve an epic love story?"

"Some of us would settle for a little hanky-panky," Mai said, lifting material from a wet bath to slap against a wooden beam. "Or hell, I'd even be happy with a guy asking me out for dinner. Do you have any idea how long it's been since I went to dinner? This town is suffering a man drought."

"It's true," Annie said, adjusting her heat pack over her abdomen. "We should all pack up and move to Miami and buy a house where we can grow old together in true *Golden Girls* style."

"FYI, I'm Dorothy," Mai said, rubbing sweat from her forehead. "Frankie's Blanche—of course."

"Of course," I said, nodding sagely.

"Does that make me Rose?" Flo asked.

"Do you even have to ask?"

"Wait, I'm Sophia?" Annie cried, pressing a hand to her chest in mock horror. "How dare you. How absolutely *dare* you."

I sniggered.

"But back to Frankie." Mai laid the material over the beam, turning to the camera fully. "Babe, what does your heart say?"

I paused, taking my time to consider the question as objectively as I could.

"That he's trying. That even if I end up heartbroken, taking a chance on what could be a great relationship isn't a loss."

Annie grimaced as she shifted uncomfortably in her chair. "Okay, I'm temporarily on board the Jay train. But I reserve the right to cancel my ticket at any time."

"Does this mean Frankie's getting herself some *wood*?" Mai asked slyly.

"*Wooden* that be nice?"

"I'd say she's an expert at *whittling* down his—"

I groaned, dropping my head into my hands. "You guys are the worst."

My cell buzzed.

"Is that the man of the hour?" Mai asked.

I glanced at the screen, my grin instantaneous.

"Oh my God it is! Flo, this bitch has a naughty smile on her face!"

Flo giggled, the sound delicate and beautiful. "I can't wait to dance at their wedding."

"I'm logging off," I told them sternly. "Goodbye."

I cut their laughter short, looking down at Jay's text feeling all warm and gooey at the sight of his name on my screen.

"Be warned, Jay Wood. I'm going to friend-date the shizz out of you."

## 16

**Jay**

I pulled into Frankie's drive, anticipation simmering my blood.

"Of course, she has a pink door."

I grabbed my bag, shrugging it on as I headed up her walk. Sadly devoid of any life-sized dinosaurs, the only pops of colour came from painted raised garden beds and a cluster of bright but wilting sunflowers.

Very un-Frankie.

I pressed her doorbell just as Frankie yanked the pink door open.

"Don't—damn. Too late."

The chime rang out a familiar tune.

"Is that 'WAP'?"

She sighed heavily, stray hairs flying. "Annie did it. I can't figure out how to change it back. I had to convince my mother WAP meant 'we all party'. I strongly suspect I failed."

A grin stole across my face, my body reacting to the sight of her. Today she wore a loose cream blouse, her shoulders bare, her riot of pink hair falling freely down her back and collarbone. Powder blue jeggings encased her legs and matched her fresh nail polish with pink Converse completing her outfit.

"You're wearing a tie."

I looked down, smoothing the navy fabric over my favourite printed t-shirt. "So I am."

"Is this a fashion statement? Because I'm not sure it's working for you."

I closed the gap between us, standing directly in front of her chair. "Grab it."

She frowned but fisted the fabric.

"Our heights are too different for you to randomly kiss me. Now, when you want to lay one on me, you can grab and pull."

For a moment she stared at me, a flush touching her cheeks.

"I don't know whether to be offended or flattered you're essentially wearing a dog collar."

I chuckled. "Flattered. Definitely flattered."

She gently tugged on the tie. I curled down until we were face-to-face.

"As convenient as you think this is, don't do it again. If I want to kiss you, you'll know."

"Oh?" I waggled my eyebrows. "Will there be a secret sign? A code word, perhaps?"

"Jay?"

"Mm?"

She crooked her finger at me and I leaned in, eager for a taste of her.

The infuriating woman slid said finger between us, my lips pressing against her hand instead of her mouth.

"See? You'll know." She laughed at my disgruntled

expression, hands dropping to her push rims to roll herself backward. "Come on, friend. Let me show you the studio."

I'd expected her house to be a riot of colour—every wall a different shade. I should have known Frankie wasn't any ordinary rainbow—she was the classy kind where you found a pot of gold at one end, and her house reflected her perfectly.

Between white walls and wood tile floors lay a cacophony of colour. Pink sofas, blue cabinetry, yellow curtains. Watercolours and vibrant framed prints drew the eye. Figurines of different feminist icons were placed here and there, a Ruth Bader Ginsberg statue holding pride of place on her mantel.

Apart from RBG's hair, there wasn't a scrap of grey or beige to be seen.

"Nice place."

"Thanks. My landlord is cool, but the HOA is a nightmare. You know they won't let me plant anything but flowers? I had all these grand plans for seasonal vegetables and got hit with a fine." She shook her head. "But finding accessible housing in the Cove is a nightmare so here I am, staying until I can afford to buy."

"Accessible housing?"

"Mmhm. No steps, accessible toilet—preferably with support bars. A shower I can leave a chair in. Low kitchen counters, that kind of thing."

Frankie threw out her needs as easily as talking about the weather—and why not? They were as much a part of her life as the sun and moon. I might run kink classes and help people work out how to make bondage accessible, but I'd just been schooled in how much I didn't know about dating someone with disability.

"This way, the studio's through the bedroom." She pushed her door open, leading me into her personal space.

I'd stroked myself last night to thoughts of her sprawled across pink sheets. But taking in the rich forest green bedspread, the abundance of indoor plants, and the dark and moody nude hanging above her bed, my fantasy shattered in the best of ways.

"That's—" I cleared my throat. "That's you."

"Uh-huh. Mai took it for a class last year." Frankie stopped, looking up at the image of herself sprawled across her wheelchair, her hair covering her breasts, a soft draping fabric falling between her legs and hiding her core from view.

"She got top marks for it, too." Frankie pushed off, rolling toward a door on the far side of the room. "This way."

I stared at the black-and-white nude portrait for a beat longer, committing to memory the curves of her body, the shape of her breasts, her slightly parted lips.

My cock pressed against my fly as blood rushed to my dick, need pulsing through me.

*I want to taste her.*

"Jay?"

I forced my gaze from the picture, finding Frankie watching me.

"You're fucking gorgeous."

She flushed, her gaze boldly holding mine. "And you're going to make us late in submitting the recording. You can worship me later."

"Friends," I choked out, stumbling after her. "We're meant to be friend dating."

"Frating is overrated."

Her walk-in closet had been transformed into a recording booth. Microphones, lights, and cameras were positioned around the space, the walls lined with sound-proofing foam.

"Why the cameras? Isn't this a podcast?"

"Yep, but we post the videos so anyone who is deaf or hard of hearing can access it. We add captions and there's a downloadable transcript every week too."

"We?"

"Chrissy."

She gestured for me to take a seat, rolling into place on the other side of the desk.

"How's this all work?" I asked, dropping my bag on the ground beside me.

"You pop the earphones on, speak into the microphone, and answer questions."

I rolled my eyes. "You know, I should begin spanking you for these snarky comments."

She perked up. "How would that work for someone without much feeling in their lower extremities? Is that something you have experience with? Wait, let me start recording."

I chuckled. "Frankie, slow down. We've got all night. Besides." I gestured at my bag. "You said you wanted to focus on rope for this episode."

"True. We should cover spanking next time."

"There'll be a next time?"

She sent me a flirty grin. "If you play your cards right, anything is possible."

Fuck. This woman had me questioning my stupid no-sex decree.

Experience had taught me sex messed up relationships. It was why I'd suggested the rule. Sex clouded your vision and blinded you to who the person really was—and for some reason, I *needed* Frankie to know the real me.

*To want the real me.*

How fucked up was that?

I couldn't think on why I needed this so badly—if I dwelled on it, I'd go crazy.

Introspection could wait, Frankie deserved all my attention.

## 17

**Frankie**

"Ready?"

Jay nodded, green eyes sparkling with good humour as he watched me lean toward the microphone.

"And three, two, one." I hit record, shooting him a wink.

"Hello and welcome to the *All Access* podcast. I'm your host, Frankie Kenton, here to talk about sex, access, and everything in between. Today we have a special guest with us to discuss accessible bondage. I don't know about you, but I'm freaking excited!"

I hit a button, my jingle playing through the head-phones. Jay raised his hands, giving a little shimmy in his seat, his grin pulling his short beard wide.

A pulsing ache began to build low in my abdomen, arousal heating my blood. I wanted to toss off the earphones and push him onto my bed. I wanted to lick him from top to toe.

*Thirsty? Baby, I was parched.*

"I'm joined today by Jay who teaches accessible bondage. Jay, welcome to the podcast."

"Great to be here."

"Tell us a little about yourself. How did you become a rigger? How did you discover bondage?"

I couldn't explain the change but it was as if a mask dropped over him. Out went laughing, funny, adorable Jay and in his place sat sexy Jay—master of ropes, prince of my pussy.

Or, at least I hoped he would be.

"I watched my first scene in Italy. I can't remember exactly how I ended up at this kink party but I went and watched shibari for the first time." His green eyes flashed, his body taking on the relaxed tension of a tiger watching his prey. "And I knew I wanted to study it."

"Did you have much experience with rope before viewing the scene?"

He shook his head. "Not beyond my job. I've worked with my dad since high school. We own a lumber yard and a handful of forest plantations around America." His lips quirked. "And working in a lumber yard or on the farms means working with ropes which I enjoyed—probably more than I should have."

Images of Jay chopping wood hurled through my head, a lumbersexual fantasy beginning to take shape. In his battered work boots, graphic shirt, and worn jeans, Jay looked more rocker than lumberjack, but add some plaid and an axe and I could see how the guy would transform from scruffy rocker to rugged mountain man.

"So, you discovered your love via work?"

His dark gaze met mine. "I'd say it found me."

I swallowed, my blood heating. "And accessibility?"

"When I returned to Capricorn Cove, I started

attending The A-List. It's a local kink club run by a couple who have lived experience with disability. They were in the scene but found a lot of the clubs weren't supporting people with disabilities. There were issues with accessibility for equipment, sensory overload, that kind of thing. Frustrated, they opened their own place catering to everyone."

"And you teach classes there?"

"Mm." Jay shifted forward, leaning his forearms on the desk. "I started teaching as a way to give back to the community. Finding safe ways to play can sometimes be a challenge—and we both know I enjoy a challenge."

Goosebumps dimpled my skin, my body giving a small shiver.

We talked about his accessible classes discussing the types of issues beginners should consider, common questions, and where my listeners could find more information.

"Alright, I have to ask." I sent him a teasing smile. "What is it about the ropes in particular that you enjoy?"

He leaned back, crossing his arms over his chest, the fingers of his left hand beginning to stroke his right bicep, the movement slow and hypnotic.

Jay tipped his head to one side, giving me a long, filthy once-over.

"The trust," he said slowly, his voice taking on a rough tone. "A bunny is giving themselves into your care. They're entrusting you with their safety, with their pleasure, with their body. You control every part of the scene from the rope type to the ties to the length of the scene." His voice dropped an octave. "It's your duty to fulfil their needs—and that's a heady thing for me."

My body pulsed—my nipples too sensitive, my skin overheated. I ached for him to touch me. I throbbed to be under his hand, to experience that same strange freedom that came from being bound.

I barely recognised my voice as I asked, "But for you, it's often not about sex?"

He nodded. "Kink isn't just about an orgasm. The act can add to sexual pleasure, but sometimes it's less about the sex and more about the release. You're stirring feelings up in the other person. You're giving them what they're searching for —for some that's a sexual release. For others, it's physical or mental freedom."

I thought back to my experience on the mat and what stood out—the feel of Jay's hands on me, the ropes pressing against my skin, and his constant direction and praise.

"I think I understand," I said slowly. "When you bound me, I thought I'd feel trapped. But there was a freedom in it. You were giving me permission to live in the moment. You took everything away from me which forced me to just feel. It's not something I've experienced before."

"Did you like it?"

I nodded. "Very much."

"Would you do it again?"

The question floated in the space between us, big and scary.

*Would I?*

I took my time answering, pulling out my tangled feelings, examining each emotion one by one—determined to ensure my attraction to Jay didn't cloud my decision.

*Would I do it again?*

I thought of the scene, noting my body's reaction. Muscles tensed, butterflies took flight in my stomach, my heart began to pound, my pulse jumping.

I raised my head, my gaze locking with Jay's.

"Yes."

## 18

**Jay**

W*hat the fuck am I doing?*

Frankie's unequivocal yes left me wanting. My hands itched to run over her body, words forming on the tip of my tongue as my mind mapped out our next scene.

Kink could be done without sex. I'd done it before. Hell, when working with Lea on the accessible demonstrations there wasn't a whisper of sexual attraction between the two of us.

I could do this. I *would* do this.

"Get on the bed."

Frankie stared at me, her tongue flicking out to lick her lips. "What about your boundaries?"

"Get on the bed."

She moved backward, her gaze still locked with mine. "You're sure?"

"Get on the fucking bed, Frankie. Now."

I watched her shudder at my command, her cheeks flushing. "Yes, sir."

I knew she meant it as a flippant comment, but the breathy need threading through her voice lent it cadence, drawing us both into the scene.

I waited for her to leave before standing and lifting my rope bag. I turned then hesitated for a moment.

"Fuck it."

I snatched one of the wireless microphones from the desk, following her into the bedroom.

Frankie pulled out a slide board, transitioning from her chair to the side of the bed. She tipped her head back, waiting for my next order.

*Good girl.*

"Get in the middle." I placed the microphone on her bedside table, dropping my bag on the floor. "You need any supports?"

She shook her head, hands braced on either side of her.

"Close your eyes."

She drew in a breath, her eyelids fluttering shut as I moved around the room, heading for her en suite. Inside, I scrubbed my hands then filled the sink with warm water, dropping a wash cloth in to soak.

"Jay, what are you—"

"Quiet, babe."

I dried my hands, returning to the room. Frankie sat on the bed, her body tense, legs stretched out before her, hands fisting the covers.

The zipper of my bag sounded loud in the hushed quiet. I withdrew a length of cotton rope running it through my fingers.

"I ordered new ropes and washed them when they arrived." I held up the length dragging it over her exposed skin. "I want to use this on you, Frankie." I leaned over the bed to stroke knuckles along her cheek. "But I want you naked for this experience."

Her eyelids fluttered then slammed shut, her lips parting as a flush worked its way up her neck.

"You're sure?"

I glanced up at the nude photo above her bed. It hung like an appetiser to the glory of her body.

"Fuck yes."

She nodded, her mouth opening but no words escaping.

"Look at me, Frankie."

She blinked her eyes open.

"Say it," I ordered. "I need to know you want this."

"I do. I want you to strip me naked. I want you to tie me up." She bit her lower lip. "I want you to make me come."

*Fuck.*

I tossed the length of rope on the bed. "Good girl."

I snatched up one of her hair ties scattered on her bedside table, sliding it onto my wrist. I sitting on the bed, I shifted behind Frankie, my hands skimming over her clothing and up her sides. I nuzzled my face into her neck pressing lingering kisses against her sensitive skin.

"Jay."

My name had never sounded so fucking good.

My hands slipped into her locks, gently brushing through them, slowly shifting the bulk to her back.

"You did this last time," she whispered.

"And I'll do it again," I promised, gathering her hair into a ponytail. I tied it off and began to stroke hands down the sides of her neck, over her shoulders, and down her back. I watched goose bumps rise on her skin, watched her breath catch and ease, watched her shudder and shimmer, cataloging each reaction for further examination.

My fingers tangled in the bottom of her shirt, slipping under to stroke the soft skin at her hips.

"I'm gonna peel these clothes from your body, rainbow. I'm going to kiss every inch of your skin as I bind you. I'm gonna make you feel so fucking good."

She shuddered against my hands, stiffening as I slowly drew her shirt up revealing her to my hungry gaze.

"Hands up," I whispered against her ear, using my chest to brace her.

She raised them slowly and I pulled off her shirt tossing it to the side. With her hands braced on the bed, I shifted, moving around until I could crouch over her legs, my gaze dancing over the abundance before me.

I unclipped her bra, stripping it from her body, gratified when her breasts bounced free. Unable to resist, I leaned in, tasting the sweetness of her pert nipple, teasing her with my tongue.

Her hands fluttered up, burying in my hair.

I drew back, barking out an order. "Hands at your sides."

She dropped them, a little whimper escaping her.

I rewarded her with a kiss to her shoulder, nipping at the sensitive skin. "Good girl."

My fingers slipped into the elastic waistband of her jeggings. "Do you need to lift up or lay back?"

"I'll lift up."

She repositioned herself, her strong arms and core forcing her body up. I slid the jeggings and underwear down, letting her settle back on the bed before removing them completely. Smooth skin greeted my touch, my fingers running along her legs.

"I can't feel you," Frankie whispered, her gaze locked on the hand currently cupping her knee.

"But you see what I'm doing." I ran my hands further up

her legs. "And I can feel you. I feel your soft skin. I feel your delicate limbs, and I watch how my words are turning you on."

She huffed out a quiet laugh. "This shouldn't turn me on."

"The Doctor is being schooled? How strange."

She stuck out her tongue and I leaned in, nipping her lips then soothing away the sting with a kiss.

"Ready?"

She nodded, her blue eyes wide.

Pressing kisses over every available inch of her beautiful curves, I reached for the rope. Already looped, I doubled it and slipped it over her head, quickly weaving a knot between her shoulder blades.

Frankie shuddered as I moved around her, hands gliding over her skin, mouth tasting her lips, her collarbone, her shoulders, her breasts as I crafted knot after knot down the length of her front. Tying the first harness off, I rocked back on my heels, reaching for another rope.

"Another?" Frankie asked, watching my hands begin to form knots in the length.

"Mm," I murmured, checking the fit against her body. "This one goes under you."

I threaded it through the harness at her front, pulling the length down until the knots pressed against her belly. With a grin, I shifted, dropping the remaining length in her lap.

"I'm going to spread you, rainbow. I'm gonna open you to me and press one of these knots nice and tight against your clit. Then I'm gonna bind your hands and leave you to enjoy the feel of it working you."

Her breath caught, her skin flushing.

My hands dropped to her left leg. "You good with that?"

She nodded, her eyes drifting closed as I moved first one leg, then the other, spreading her wide.

"Fuck me," I groaned, catching sight of her sweet pussy. "You've got a piercing."

The little barbell rested above her clit, glinting at me, taunting me.

"Sorry not sorry," Frankie murmured, her head tipping back, her eyes still closed.

"Just for that I'm gonna have to tease you some more."

I shifted between her legs, my fingers grazing up her inner thighs, learning where her sensation began and ended.

"There," she murmured. "And there. And—" She sucked in a breath. "There, definitely there."

I grinned, circling back to tease her again and again, discovering new spots and memorising the pressure level, touch, or kiss that drove her wild. My fingers danced close to her slit then away, never quite giving her what she wanted.

I built Frankie's need, weaving her higher until my own arousal hit a fever pitch.

"Jay," she panted, her hands fisting the bed. "Touch me."

"No." I moved back, gathering the knotted rope.

"Please?"

"No." I quickly bound her, positioning the final knot a whisper below her clit. When she moved, the knot would shift up while her circular barbell would press down from the top pinching her clit. I had a feeling Frankie would adore the rough sensation.

I shifted, enjoying her gasp as I purposefully grazed the rope across her breasts.

"Jay...."

I bent, rasping my beard over first one, then her other nipple, gliding my mouth across her pert little tits.

"Oh, fuck you," Frankie cursed, shifting forward, groaning as the knot pressed tight against her, rubbing in time with her movement. "You bastard."

I chuckled, grazing my teeth over her nipple. "Not good?"

"You know it is." Her hips rocked, a low moan escaping her as the knot rubbed her clit. "Oh, God."

I skimmed my hand down her body to swirl a finger through her wet heat, relishing the evidence of her arousal. I lifted my hand to my mouth, Frankie's gaze turning to blue fire as I licked her taste clean from my fingers.

"Fucking delicious," I growled, reaching out to capture the back of her neck and pull her forward, our mouths colliding together in hungry passion.

"Jay," Frankie panted against my mouth as I worked the knot against her clit. "Why are you wearing clothes?"

I huffed out a self-deprecating laugh. "No sex, remember?"

Her gaze crashed into mine. "Aren't you going to come?"

"Nope."

"But you're going to look after me?"

"What do you think, rainbow?" I pressed the knot against her clit, enjoying her gasping moan.

"That's not fair," she panted. "You should get something too."

"I'm good."

"No, Jay. I want you to come on my tits."

I froze. "Fuck."

"Please?"

My cock pressed against my fly, my control pushed to the limit.

"No."

She looked at me, her big eyes pleading. "Pretty please with me on top?"

"Fuck." I shifted, ripping my shirt free. "Fuck."

I fumbled with my zipper, roughly shoving my jeans down, my cock bouncing free. I heard Frankie's sharp intake, gratified to find her staring at my dick.

"Oh, God," she muttered, licking her lips. "You're thick. You're so fucking thick. Jay, you're killing me."

"The feeling is entirely mutual."

She lifted a hand, reaching for my cock but dropped it back to the bed, fisting the cover.

"Good girl," I praised.

Gently guiding her back, I adjusted the bedding until she lay against the pillows, her legs spread, her delicious body open to me.

"You're a sorceress," I told her, kissing my way down to her abdomen. "You're bewitching me, Frankie. You're stealing my control. I don't get topped—ever. And yet here you are, demanding things I can't deny you."

I peppered kisses down to her pussy, my tongue sliding along the side of the rope, roughly licking and stroking Frankie's sweet cunt, her greedy moans urging me on.

"Harder," she begged. "I need more—yes! Like that!"

I fisted my cock, stroking it as I worked her hot little body.

Above me, Frankie arched, her hands reaching down to tangle in my hair, forcing my mouth to her as she came.

*Fuck, yes.*

I surged up, jerking my dick to the sight of her flushed and spent, her sated gaze watching me fuck myself.

"Fuck! Frankie." I broke, pumping my cock again and again, my cum painting her breasts in hot splashes.

Spent, I shifted to her side, running gentle hands over Frankie's heated skin as I removed her bindings. I dropped the lengths in my bag on my way to the bathroom, retrieving the warm washcloth.

Returning to the bed, I laid it against Frankie's abdomen, taking care of my gorgeous woman.

*My woman? What the fuck?*

I wanted to deny the possessive ache settling in my ribcage, wanted to reject the overwhelming need burning in my gut. But looking down at her gorgeous body my denials faded away, leaving only truth—this woman made me want things I didn't have any business wanting.

"I'll do it," she said, lifting up and holding out a hand. "You're not my carer."

"No, but I am your—" I hesitated, searching for the word. "My?"

I gave in. "Yours."

She melted, her gaze warming. "Even being mine doesn't mean you're responsible for this."

"Aftercare," I told her primly. "Is a core part of a good scene. And that *is* my responsibility." I playfully slapped away her fingers, shaking my head. "You need to learn better kink etiquette."

She chuckled, flopping back on the mattress. "Alright, take care of me. Nothing could be less sexy."

I looked down at her wealth of pink and cream skin, the taste of her still sweet on my tongue, the erotic scene we'd shared on loop.

"Rainbow, you couldn't be more wrong."

## 19

Frankie

We lay on my rumpled bed, our bodies cooling, spooned together like long-time lovers. Jay couldn't seem to stop touching me. Despite our passion having been spent, he ran lazy hands across my back, his fingers brushing lightly against the raised scars running the length of my spine.

"Spinal cancer," I said, answering his unspoken question. "I was three."

Jay's fingers stilled on my back.

"Moody for a toddler, always crying. My parents were at their wits' end. They couldn't work out why I was constantly upset. One day I fell and hit my head. They rushed me to the hospital and found the tumours. Turns out I'd been in horrible pain for months."

I paused, wondering if this might be a step too far in our relationship.

"All of these are from childhood?" Jay asked, lightly touching my scar tissue.

"No. They're from the multiple surgeries I've had in the decades since. The cancer is gone, but my spine is wrecked, the bones brittle. I've had spinal fusions and disc replacements in an effort to maintain my remaining mobility."

"That sucks."

"Yeah, it does. But I'm lucky. Some of my nerves are destroyed but others are fully functional. I can get around." I tossed him a grin over my shoulder. "I can experience orgasms, and I have some feeling in places. You take your wins where you get them."

"Do you need more operations?"

"Maybe. Not at the moment though."

We were both quiet, Jay's hands tracing the scars.

"Does it hurt?"

I chuckled, dropping my head back on the pillow. "Annie would tell you pain is relative. Is today a good pain day? Hell yes. Will tomorrow be?" I sighed. "Who knows."

"I wouldn't know from looking at you."

"Chronic pain is something you learn to deal with. Constantly telling people about it gets tiresome. Who wants to hear that? Well," I chuckled. "Except for Mai, Flo, and Annie."

"Why them?"

"They all have lived experience with disability. We met in high school thanks to a bad pizza in the cafeteria, but we bonded because of our experiences. Talking to people who have some concept of what you're dealing with can be freeing. You empathise because you get it."

Jay's fingers returned, slowly caressing my back, his rough calluses scraping pleasurably along my skin.

"Does this freak you out?" I asked softly.

"No. I'm just sorry the pain takes up space in your body joy should fill."

I looked over my shoulder. "Pain and joy aren't mutually exclusive. I can feel one while experiencing the other."

"You're an incredible woman, Frankie Kenton."

I let his praise sink deep into my bones.

He nuzzled my shoulder, pressing little kisses to my skin. "You said you liked the freedom that came from relinquishing control. Why?"

I closed my eyes, leaning into him. "So much of my life is regimented. Constrained. I'm always bound by some rule or barrier—it's exhausting. When I relinquish control, when I give it over to you, it's as if...." I trailed off, searching for the words.

"As if?" Jay prompted quietly.

"As if I'm free. I feel light, unburdened. I don't have to think, don't have to worry. You take all of that away and give me permission to simply feel."

I twisted my head, our gazes meeting. "Thank you, Jay. Without you, I'd have never experienced how empowering it is to trust someone enough to give over to them."

He cupped my cheek, leaning forward to press his forehead against mine. "You're giving me praise where none's due. It's all you, rainbow. It's always been all you."

He captured my lips, the kiss sweet and lingering.

"Frankie?"

"Mm?"

"Lay back. I need to taste you again."

He helped me roll onto my back, gently nipping at my fingers, heat pooling between my thighs.

"What if I want to taste you?" I asked.

"Then have at it."

Little fires ignited along my skin burning through my body until nothing but desire and need remained.

Jay's cock pressed against my hip, hard and hot. I

reached down, my hand circling his length, my thumb running over the crown of his cock.

With a muttered curse, he dropped his head, his lips capturing mine in a brutal kiss. There was no finesse, nothing but desperate, aching need. My mouth opened to allow his tongue to tangle with mine, delighting in his taste.

There were no ropes this time, and their absence made it hard to view this interaction as anything but a fling.

"Jay," I panted my body liquid fire. "Wait. You said no sex. I know I pushed you before, but have you—?"

"Fuck it." He shifted to nip at my earlobe, sucking the sting away. "Fuck everything I've ever said. I was a fucking idiot." He pulled back slightly, his green eyes dancing. "And right now I'm gonna make love to you."

My heart beat a rapid tattoo as he ripped away the thin veneer of distance that had existed between us. My head recognised what a stupid idea it was to get involved with him, but my body wanted his.

And my heart?

God, it had been so fucking long since anyone had come close to making me feel the way he did. If I wasn't careful, he'd be stealing it clean away.

Jay shifted back, one hand moving my legs wide, his other running down my side and across my abdomen to tangle in my curls.

His mouth continued to fuck mine, his thick, blunt fingers stroking the sensitive skin of my labia, teasing at my slit. His rough calluses scraped against me as he parted my flesh, the texture of his hands adding to my pleasure as he began to work my clit, one finger playing with my piercing while the other rubbed rough circles.

"Oh, fuck," I groaned, nails scraping down his back. "Jay!"

He worked me, concentrating on learning my tempo and

rhythm. My orgasm began to build inside me, dark and dangerous, skirting on the edge of pleasure-pain.

I arched, a gut-wrenching groan tearing from deep in my soul.

"Fuck," Jay muttered, nipping at my neck, his lips sucking the sting away. "Frankie."

He fucked me with his fingers, slipping first one, then another into me, his thumb setting a counter rhythm on my clit. Desperate gasps and harsh demands ripped from my throat, as he finger-fucked me, finding my G-spot. My right hand fisted his cock, my left leaving scratch marks down his back.

"Fuck," I groaned, stroking his dick. "I wish you were in me."

For a beat, Jay froze.

I loosened my grip. "Jay? Shit did I cross a line? Damn, I'm sorry, I—"

"Fuck it."

He ripped himself away dodging my hands as I reached out, trying to pull him back.

"Jay!"

He rolled off the bed, hitting the floor with a loud thump. I shuffled to the side of the bed, peering over to see him searching through his rope bag, dumping equipment on the floor.

"What are you—?"

"Found it!" He held the condom box up in triumph.

"You idiot." I collapsed back against the bed, a hand pressed to my thundering heart. "I thought you were abandoning me."

"Never," he promised. "First I'm gonna taste this pussy." He cupped me with one hand. "Then I'm gonna fuck you until you're feeling me for the next week."

"Promises, promises."

He climbed back on the bed, settling between my thighs —his hot breath brushing against overly sensitive skin. Gentle fingers parted me, his tongue delving to find my piercing, a rumble of pleasure slipping from his throat.

I fisted his hair, stifling cries when Jay slipped fingers inside me, stretching my slick channel until he found my G-spot once more, pressing and rubbing to send tight spirals coursing through my body.

"So fucking wet," he murmured. "Good girl."

He worked, fucking me with fingers and tongue. Unable to defend against his sensual onslaught, I exploded, clenching and undulating as I tripped over the edge into the dark abyss.

With a rough grunt, Jay surged up my body, condomed cock in hand, his gaze locked on mine as he roughly pumped his dick.

"Come here," I said, sliding my hands up to cup my breasts, pinching my nipples with a breathy moan. "Come fuck me."

## Jay

I shifted, pressing the crown of my cock against her.

"Fuck you're gorgeous."

She coloured, the flush painting her cheeks and breasts pink, her body a feast for my eyes.

"You gonna watch or play?" she asked, one hand falling from her breasts to slide over her stomach and down to tangle in her curls. "I can live with either option."

"Play." I snatched her hand, pushing it over her head and

holding it there. My head bent, my lips a whisper from hers. "Next time I'll watch you flick your pretty clit." I began to ease my cock into her, her pussy gripping me like a vice. "But this time I want to feel you squirming around me as you come."

Her breath caught, her head tipping backward as a low keening sound slipped from between her lips.

I let her adjust, determined to wring every ounce of pleasure from this moment.

"More," Frankie breathed, her nails digging into my back. "Harder, Jay. I need—"

I fucked into her, driving my cock into her tight pussy, stretching her around me, forcing myself into her slick wet heat. I pressed kisses up her collarbone, across her throat, sucking her earlobe and nipping at her chin. Frankie's fingernails scratched across my back and ass, slipping between us to pinch my nipples. Her mouth spilled filthy words of praise.

I found her lips, kissing her hard and hot, our mouths fucking as our bodies clashed, her pussy holding me captive. I worked a hand between us, snaking it down to flick her clit.

Overcome, Frankie screamed, teeth biting into my shoulder, her body pure heaven as it milked my cock.

"Fuck!"

I lost control, thrusting into her, marking her, losing my mind with the fucking incredible feel of her.

*Mine.*

We collapsed in a tangle of limbs, our bodies still fused together, sweat cooling on our skin.

"Well," Frankie murmured a few minutes later. "That was...."

I lifted my head when she didn't finish. "Excellent? Mind-blowing? Incredible? The best you've ever had?"

"Definitely the opposite of no sex."

I snorted, rolling off her to flop onto the bed. "I think we can safely call it."

"Mm?"

"Frating is out." I waved my hands around dismissively. "I was an idiot, I can see that now. It was a stupid fucking idea to think we could just be friends. Why didn't you stop me?"

She laughed, lifting up to roll her eyes. "Because you're impossible?"

"Mm, that's true." I leaned in to nip at her lips. "Alright, no more stupidity. Let's call it. We're dating." I booped her on the nose. "I'll even let you name my triceratops."

Frankie's laughter filled the room, weaving under my skin.

"You're an idiot," she said, sitting up with a groan.

"But?" I asked, hopefully.

She shuffled to the side of the bed, transitioning into her wheelchair.

"But," she called over her shoulder as she moved to the bathroom. "If you stay for dinner and finish the podcast episode, I might say yes to letting you be my boyfriend." She sent me a grin.

"You've got a deal."

An unfamiliar but pleasant feeling settled in my chest, taking up space.

"Well shit," I muttered, staring at the closed bathroom door. "I think I might be falling in love."

## 20

Jay

"I don't want to say I told you so but all evidence suggests...." Ren trailed off, his teeth flashing before he smothered his grin. "I may have been more than a little right."

We were back on the basketball court, our Wednesday afternoon session brought forward by an hour so I could get to Frankie's for another podcast recording. After the last session—which Frankie had been forced to cut everything that began with me ordering her onto the bed and finished with us eating pasta on said bed—Chrissy had requested three additional episodes exploring different kinks and their accessibility options.

I'd agreed—on the proviso Frankie first tried every option.

She'd laughed, patting me on the arm. "Oh, Jay. How you underestimate me. When do we start?"

The woman had carved a Frankie-shaped hole in my heart before I'd even had a chance to think about erecting barriers. While working, her podcast played in my ears. I found myself thinking of her far more often than I should, wondering if she thought of me, wanting the taste of her on my tongue.

*I've got it bad.*

I threw Ren a salty look. "You don't have to rub it in. I shouldn't need to justify myself to you."

"Uh-huh." Ren began to dribble the ball. "And what are you and the lovely Frankie getting up to tonight?"

"We're recording another episode."

"And?"

"And we might get dinner."

"Uh-huh."

"Uh-huh?" I asked, echoing him. "Uh-huh. What the fuck does uh-huh mean?"

"Nothing. It's a nothing word. It's like fine." Ren tapped a finger against his chin. "Fine is also a nothing sound. How are you? Fine. How's the weather? Fine. How was the wedding? Fine. See? Nothing words."

I snorted, flipping him the bird. "Liar. Have you thought about going to law school? 'Cause you're passing judgment left, right, and centre, buddy."

He tossed me the ball. "If I'm Judge Judy, what does that make you? The defendant?"

I dodged around him, scoring a three-pointer. "Piss poor retort, Ren."

"Hey, cut me some slack, I'm coming off two twenty-four-hour shifts." He yawned wide enough to crack his jaw, one hand scrubbing at the dark circles under his eyes. "Shit, I'm beat."

I tucked the ball under my arm. "Go home. The twins bailed, maybe it's time for you to do the same."

He chuckled, crossing his arms over his chest. "And the

fact you could head to Frankie's early has absolutely nothing to do with this generous offer?"

I tossed him the ball, gratified when he doubled over with an "oof."

"Go get some sleep. And stop gossiping. You're worse than my stepmom—God bless Karen—but the woman loves a good gossip."

Ren laughed, turning on his heel. "I'll see you next week. Have fun with Ms. Kenton."

"Doctor!" I yelled after him. "She's *Doctor* Kenton!"

He sent me a satisfied grin over his shoulder, collecting his bag. "I know."

"Motherfucker."

I pulled out my cell to shoot a text off to Frankie.

"Hey, Jay?"

I looked up to find Ren watching me from the entrance to the court, one hand on the door, the other holding his backpack.

"What? Decided you *do* want an ass-kicking?"

He slowly shook his head. "Look, you probably don't want me to say anything but we all know McKenzie did a number on you. She fed you lies and convinced you of shit that has never been remotely true."

I flinched, the mere mention of McKenzie like a sucker punch to the gut.

"And I know you don't speak about her or that night —ever."

I opened my mouth to dismiss his claim but the words wouldn't come.

"She was wrong. And Frankie's your proof."

I cleared my throat, trying for flippancy and failing. "Get to the point."

He shrugged. "You look happy, dude. Now, I'm not normally one to stick my nose in—"

I snorted.

"—but seriously, hang on to this one. She's a good woman to know and love. And you, my friend, deserve good in your life. I'll catch you next week."

And with his bombshell lobbed, the fucker left, leaving me to process the fallout.

"Well fuck," I muttered, running a hand through my hair. "What the fuck am I meant to do with that?"

I looked down at my cell, shoving aside Ren and the bullshit he'd stirred up.

JAY

> Basketball finished early. I'm claiming victory. Pizza and beer to go with your next kink class?

FRANKIE

> If you're buying. But this is the truest test of our relationship so far…. What toppings will you order?

JAY

> Toppings? You have toppings? What's wrong with cheese?

Her reply came through as I stepped from the shower.

FRANKIE

> You better be joking right now or there will be a murder. You think I'm lying? I know where to bury bodies, don't test me.

I didn't know how to categorise these interactions. My previous experience with women usually involved thinly veiled sexual innuendo followed by hookup plans—not arguing over pizza toppings.

A food-related text shouldn't turn me on just like her questions about my day shouldn't cause my chest to ache. Yet here we were.

"Ridiculous." I ran a hand over my damp beard. "This is some grade-A bullshit. I'm thirty fucking years old. I should have my shit together by now."

And yet the ghost of the girlfriend past sat heavily on my shoulders, whispering doubts in my ear.

"Frankie's not her," I muttered, yanking on my jeans. "Frankie's not even remotely like her."

I forcefully shoved the memories away, ignoring the swirling in my gut.

"Fuck Ren." I reached for my shoes. "Everything's good. Great even. Everything's fucking perfect. Absolutely perfect."

I looked down at my hands, fisting them to stop the trembling, determined to ignore the knot of anxiety twisting in my gut.

"It's fine," I muttered. "Everything is fine."

## 21

Frankie

"Don't you think it's a bit soon to be meeting his family?" Annie asked from where she lazed on my bed.

I considered myself in my bedroom mirror, fiddling with the sleeve of my dress.

The weather had finally cooled as autumn descended. Leaves were beginning to fall from trees while the scent of pumpkin spice hung in the air.

"No. We've been together for nearly two months." I paused, hugging the memories of those two glorious months close. I'd met his friends and he'd met mine. He slotted into my life and I'd discovered my place in his. It felt magical. Right. Good.

I found myself daydreaming of our future—the incredible sex, the laughs, a yard full of dinosaurs for our theoretical kids to play on. Unlike some of my previous relationships, that imagined future felt real and within reach.

Which is why it didn't make sense whenever I caught Jay staring at me with fear in his eyes.

"Besides," I continued, searching for my lipstick. "It's not all of his family—just his dad, stepmom, and their youngest kids who are still at home."

"I thought you said he didn't have a relationship with his birth parents."

"He doesn't. He calls his foster father dad."

"Oh, so you're not meeting anyone important."

I chuckled at her dry tone. "You're in a mood today."

In typical Annie fashion her bun had slipped free, hair flying around her head like a blonde halo. She wore black jeans and a branded shirt with her S#!T Happens logo over her left breast. She'd come directly from a meeting with her supplier which I could tell from the deep V between her eyebrows and the clench of her jaw, hadn't gone well.

"I'm stressed and PMS-ing, you're going to have to deal with bitchy Annie."

"And that's a change how?"

A pillow slapped me in the back of my head.

"Hey!"

"Hey yourself." She sobered. "Frankie, are you sure about him? You've never been to his house."

"*In* his house," I corrected. "I've dropped him off plenty of times."

"Kissing in the driveway of his discount Jurassic Park doesn't count."

I rolled my eyes. "He has stairs, Annie. It's not like I can just stroll on in."

Annie snorted. "Five stairs to his porch. You're telling me he couldn't help you up them?"

"He probably could." I sighed. "But I didn't want him to."

Her golden gaze glinted dangerously, her eyes narrowing. "And why exactly would you not want that?"

*Damn it. This is the problem with friends, they know you too well.*

I muttered something under my breath.

"Oh, don't you fucking dare." She waggled a finger at me. "You better not be putting yourself down."

"I'm not. It's just—he's made me a ramp. And I kind of like that the first time I'll be inside his house didn't involve me being hauled around."

She sighed, pinching her nose. "There is so much to unpack here I don't even know where to start or if we have time."

"Can we do cliff notes?" I asked hopefully.

She dropped her hand, her face shadowed with worry. "Alright, the stairs—pride or comfort?"

"Ego," I admitted. "I'm being stubborn about it. He already does so much for me, it's a point of pride that if the ramp is in place I don't have to ask for help."

Annie nodded. "I get it. I just...."

"You're worried."

"Yeah, I am. I don't want you to get hurt."

"Why do you think I'm going to get hurt?"

She sighed, shrugging. "He's not been in a relationship in a really long time, Frankie. What does that say about him?"

I moved to the bed, reaching out to capture her hands. "Babe, what I'm about to say, I say with love. You haven't been in a relationship in a really long time either. What does that say about you?"

"That there's a man drought?" She shook her head, a small self-deprecating smile touching her lips. "I get it. I need to check my prejudice."

"You do." I squeezed her hands. "But you love me, so I get why you're worried." I hesitated. "But Annie, is this worry for me... or is it you looking for a distraction?"

She sucked in a breath. "You're psychoanalysing me."

I chuckled. "Yep. It's time. This is a conversation we have to have."

"Nope. Not today. Or ever." She jumped off the bed, snatching her tote from the floor. "Go have dinner with the parents." She pressed a kiss to my cheek. "Love you. Be a good girl. Or a bad one—whichever is more fun." She turned, heading for the door. "And tell Jay... hi."

My heart gave a happy dance at her concession. "I will."

"And ask him where he got his yard dinosaurs. I want a giant toilet roll made for my garden."

I snorted. "You're not getting a giant toilet roll."

She paused in the doorway. "Oh. I definitely one hundred per cent am."

With a last wave, she left, stomping through my house and slamming the door shut behind her—quiet and subtle were *not* in her vocabulary.

I looked back at the mirror, pursing my lips together trying to breathe through the butterflies in my stomach.

I'd only ever met two boyfriends' parents before—neither experience ended well.

First had been my high school sweetheart. His dad had spoken to me like I was deaf the whole meal then asked if I needed to be pushed to the car. We'd parted on amicable terms unrelated to his parents but it had left me gun-shy.

The last had been a guy three years ago. We'd dated casually for about two months before he'd invited me to attend a family birthday with him. His mother had stared at me for a full five minutes then burst into tears, asking him why he insisted on doing this to her. He'd been a nice guy but I wasn't content to live with that kind of shadow hanging over my relationship.

"You can do this, Frankie. Roll the dice, jump off the cliff, and let the chips fall where they may." I gave myself a final once-over then nodded firmly.

"Let's do this."

I PARKED in Jay's drive, laughing at his latest garden offering.

The dinosaurs, it seemed, liked to celebrate unusual theme days. Today they all wore beards.

Jay bounced out of the house and down to meet me at my car, holding the door open as I hauled my wheelchair across my lap.

"Hello, beautiful." He pressed an exuberant kiss to my lips. "Did you know it's World Beard Day?" He rubbed his cheeks against mine.

"Stop it, you child!"

He grinned, his gaze dipping to check me out. "You're looking particularly colourful today."

I looked down at my dress. I'd chosen to embrace the turning of the seasons and worn an autumn print scene.

"Shit, should I go change?"

Jay stared at me for a beat. "How did you get to 'I should go change' from 'you're looking colourful'?"

I huffed. "It was your tone."

"Ah." He knit his hands together, pressing his index fingers to his lips. "I see. You mistook my, I-want-to-rip-your-dress-from-your-body tone for a you're-wearing-the-wrong-thing tone." His hands did a swan dive to point down at his feet. "But I don't blame you when you are dating such a fashionista of a boyfriend."

I snorted. "Really, Jay? Sandals?"

"Your feet's best friend."

"I'm ashamed of you."

"No, you're not." He leaned in, kissing me. "You know, I expected you to have categorised all of my reactions by now." He shook his head sadly. "Worst girlfriend ever."

"Is that because she's sobered up and decided to dump you?" a young male voice asked.

I shifted, looking behind Jay to see a teenager standing in the driveway, a young girl peeking from behind his legs.

Jay clutched at his chest. "Such snark from my own brother!" He pretended to keel over. "It's a mortal wound. My heart will never recover."

I transitioned from the car, watching as the little girl ran to Jay, throwing her arms around him.

"I'll kiss you better!"

Jay scooped her up, pretending to groan as she wrapped her arms around his neck. "Look at that, I'm all fixed!" He blew a raspberry on her cheek, sending me a wink as she squealed, squirming in his arms.

*Be still thy ovaries. Thy God of spontaneous impregnation has arrived.*

"Frankie, meet Sam the sullen teenager."

The kid rolled his eyes but gave me a friendly smile.

"And this is Princess Janeane."

"Hi." I waved at the shy little girl. She hid her head in his neck, turning away from me.

"Come on in, Will and Karen have taken over the kitchen."

I pushed beside him, smiling up at Janeane when she peeked at me through her fingers.

"Are they worried you might ruin dinner?" I teased,

having discovered Jay also couldn't cook a meal to save his life.

Sam laughed behind me. "I like you."

"Thank you," I told him, trying to calm my inner excited squealing. "The feeling is mutual."

I pushed easily up the newly installed ramp, pausing to wait for Jay to open the door.

"Welcome to hell, Frankie," Sam said from behind me. "Hope your tetanus shots are up to date."

The inside of Jay's home needed work. A lot of work. There were holes in walls, faded and peeling wallpaper, and a wood floor that looked like it hadn't been touched since the dark ages.

"It's... ah... that is... I mean." I swallowed a laugh at Jay's hopeful expression. "It's got potential."

He laughed, laying a hand on the wall. "Don't listen to her, baby. She doesn't know you like I do. You're perfect just as you are."

Sam slipped past me, reaching for Janeane to place her on the ground. "We all told him not to do it but he fell in love with the dinosaurs. We suggested he buy the statues but he started rambling about not wanting to remove them from their natural habitat. Next thing we knew there were more in the front yard and a pterodactyl on order."

Janeane smiled shyly at me. "Harold is my favourite."

I leaned down until I was at her eye level. "Harold's my favourite too."

She brightened. "Do you like raptors?"

"Absolutely," I confirmed. "What's your favourite thing about them?"

She frowned thinking for a long moment then brightening. "Their teamwork. They hunt in packs and would rip you apart as a family."

I slapped my mouth shut, desperately trying to smother the hysterical laughter caught in my throat.

"Sam, do you want to take Janeane to the backyard?"

Sam nodded. "Sure. Come on, noodle."

She skipped along beside him, chatting animatedly about dinosaurs. It was only once they were out of earshot, I dared to look at Jay—finding his own mirth matched my own.

"Teamwork?" I croaked, giggles breaking free.

"She's five and already I'm fearful of her." He shook his head. "She'll either rule the world or destroy it."

"Such great power in one so young."

We both laughed.

"Well, isn't this lovely?"

I tensed, glancing over to find a couple in their mid-forties standing in the doorway watching us with identical amused expressions. I stared at them struck by a weird sense of déjà vu—and not the this-is-a-small-town-I've-seen-you-around kind of vibe but more the I-really-do-know-you feeling.

"Frankie, meet my dad, Will, and stepmom, Karen. Guys, this is Frankie."

He placed a hand on my shoulder giving me a reassuring squeeze.

Will had salt-and-pepper hair, a wide grin, and the kind of wrinkles that spoke of living a good life. Karen's head hovered a touch below his shoulder, her pile of hair adding an extra inch. Short and plump, she wore a cute wrap dress I immediately wanted in every colour and print.

"It's great to meet you." I wheeled forward, holding out a hand for them to shake.

"Oh no," Will said, holding his arms out wide. "In this family, we hug."

He shifted to the side of the chair, bending to wrap me in a quick embrace, Karen immediately taking his place to squeeze me tight.

"We're so pleased to meet you," she whispered. "So incredibly pleased."

As she pulled back it hit me.

"Holy shit!" I caught her hand. "You're Karen Q. You host the *Wicked Women* podcast!"

The three of them burst out laughing.

"Told you she'd know who you are," Jay said, throwing an arm around Karen. "You've got to face it, Karrie, you're a—" He raised a hand to punctuate his words. "—big deal."

She waved him off. "I run a podcast, that's all."

"A freaking great one." Will gestured toward the sounds of screams coming from the back of the house. "We should go rescue Sam before the Princess kills him. Frankie, would you like a drink?"

I trailed him in a daze, listening to Jay tease Karen and give Will shit.

They were a lovely family, welcoming me with open arms and open questions. There was the occasional teasing probe from Karen or Sam, but for the most part, dinner went without a hitch, and seeing Jay interact with his family did strange things to my heart.

*Strange but wonderful things.*

We sat nursing beers on Jay's back deck, stomach full of hamburgers and salad, watching Sam chase Janeane around the yard.

"Mom!" Janeane screamed, dodging Sam's half-hearted tag effort. "Jay! Come play!"

They both heaved to their feet with groans, Jay dropping a kiss to my forehead as he passed. "Be right back." He paused, turning back to wiggle a finger at his father. "Don't chase her off."

If you didn't look closely you might have assumed he'd been teasing. But I caught the flash in his eyes, the tension in his shoulders, the last lingering glance my way as he moved to play with his sister.

"Out of all my kids, he's the one I worry about the most," Will said a moment later, breaking the easy quiet between us. "He's always been the most sensitive. Covers it well by focusing the conversation back on you and cracking jokes, but I see him." He glanced my way, his gaze assessing. "I think you do as well."

I swallowed, giving one nod.

"Mm." He turned to watch the frantic game. "I know what you're thinking—how'd a spring chicken like myself end up with seven kids."

I chuckled, some of the tension loosening in my gut. "It did cross my mind."

"Hayden, my eldest, was the result of a busted condom. Pregnant at seventeen, married the same year, divorced at eighteen." He raised his beer, taking a swig. "His mom wasn't ready for kids and I wasn't ready for marriage. We parted ways and I got full custody of Hayden."

"Must have been tough."

"Sure. You're terrified for twenty-three hours out of every day and in an exhausted sleep for the other one. But I wouldn't trade it."

I watched Sam and Jay pretend to fall over, Janeane immediately jumping on them while Karrie tried to referee.

"Why fostering?"

"My parents. We lived with them for the first few years of Hayden's life and they were emergency carers. One kid, I'll never forget him, he came to us full of piss and fire ready to burn everything down." Will tipped his beer bottle toward the backyard. "When they said Jay needed a longer-term arrangement, I stuck my hand up."

"Jay said you adopted four boys?"

"Yep. My older boys are grown and off living their lives."

I looked to Jay, finding him with hands on hips, his gaze flicking between me and his dad. I raised a hand, sending him a little wave and a reassuring smile. He relaxed, blowing me a flourishing air kiss, then jumped back into the melee, allowing Janeane to tackle him to the ground.

"Why not Jay?"

"His birth mom never relinquished her parental rights. Then he aged out." Will shook his head. "Doesn't matter what his surname is, he's family."

I grinned, loving that Jay had Will's guidance in his life.

"Frankie." Will turned to me, his expression serious. "Don't take this the wrong way but there's something I need to say."

I braced, readying myself for Will's judgment.

"I know it's soon, but I sincerely hope you consider loving my boy. He's work, no doubt about it. But he'll make your life rich."

I relaxed, glancing over at the man pretending to be beaten up by a five-year-old.

"He already has."

"He's got demons. His past is a veritable minefield of triggers. But if you work hard and keep holding his hand, he'll come through the other side."

I cleared my throat. "I appreciate the heads up, but I think this is straying into a conversation that should be between Jay and I."

Will gave me an approving look. "True. I'll shut my

mouth but just want to say this—it's good to see him happy.
"

Will stood, stretching.

"Now, you any good at the wonderful game of Bullshit?"

"Never heard of it," I lied with a wink.

Will laughed. "I like you. You'll fit in just fine."

My heart full, I followed him into the house thinking the feeling was entirely mutual.

---

## 22

**Jay**

"Dad, have you seen Frankie?" I asked, tossing a kitchen towel over my shoulder as I stepped onto my back deck.

"She said she was getting something from her car," Sam called frowning at the cards in his hand. "Bullshit."

"Damn it!" Karrie slapped the cards on the table. "I give up. What am I doing wrong?"

"Your face is too honest."

I left them to it, walking around the side of the house in search of my woman, eager to share a stolen moment with her.

Rounding the house I caught sight of her on the sidewalk, pushing down the street.

"What the fuck? Frankie!"

I kicked into a run, jogging across the yard to where she'd stopped in front of my neighbour's house.

"Where are you going?"

Even in the twilight of the evening, I could see the blush on her cheeks.

"The rec centre."

Something sinister hatched in my gut, clawing its way up my spine. "Why?"

She glanced away. "I need to grab something."

*She's lying,* a voice whispered in my ear.

"Get what?" Blood rushed to my head, my voice sounding distant.

"Nothing. Just—nothing. Don't worry about it." She shifted in her chair, her face flushed. "How about you go back inside and I'll—"

"Are you meeting someone?" The question whipped out, cracking the air between us.

"What?" Her head jerked up, her gaze snapping to meet mine. "Why would you ask that?"

"Answer the question."

"No!"

"Then what are you doing? Why else would you be going to the fucking rec centre at fucking nine at night?"

"Because I need to use their accessible toilet!" She tossed the words out, her hands pointing at my house. "I can't fit in your bathroom. The chair doesn't fit and I'm not going to ask you to fucking carry me. I thought, rather than go home, maybe I could pop down to the centre with no one the wiser." She scrubbed at her face, tears glinting on her lashes. "I'm sorry. I should have told you. I—"

I crouched at her side, wrapping her in my arms, holding her close. "Fuck, Frankie. I'm so fucking sorry. I should have known better. I should have fucking realised. I measured the hall and other doorways but—fuck!"

She relaxed against me, her head resting on my shoulder. "No, it's my fault. I should have said something. I don't know why but bathrooms are a trigger for me. I let my pride get in the way of a good night."

"It's still a fucking great night." I pulled back. "Do you want me to walk you?"

"To the rec centre?" She laughed. "No, I'll be fine." She gave me a little shove. "Go distract your family for five minutes so they don't notice I'm gone and think I've abandoned them."

I stepped back, watching her wheel down the sidewalk, guilt churning in my stomach.

"I'm a fucking idiot."

"Son? You okay?"

I turned to find Will watching me from the porch, hands stuffed in his pockets.

"Do you happen to have your tools in the truck?"

Dad's eyebrows rose. "Always."

"Got a sledgehammer by any chance?"

A slow grin began to creep across his lips. "Yes."

"Great. You get yours, I'll look at the wall."

"We doing some demo?"

I glanced down the road, watching Frankie turn into the centre's parking lot.

"Yep."

**Frankie**

I returned to find Jay's truck parked on his lawn, Sam tossing plasterboard into the bed.

"What the hell happened?" I asked, staring at the load of garbage.

"Jay decided to remodel his bathroom. He's knocking the

wall down between the toilet and his bedroom." Sam lifted a shoulder in a half-shrug. "He does this sometimes. Just gets a bee in his bonnet and decides it has to happen right now. We go with it."

My heart expanded, filling my chest, a warm shimmery feeling settling in my bones.

Sam looked me over, tossing a piece of wood in the bed. "You think you can swing a hammer?"

I grinned. "I can. I'm also able to cart garbage and am occasionally known to moonlight as a cleaner."

He grinned. "Want to clean my room?"

"Not on your life, buddy. I have a brother. I'm well aware of the biohazard breeding in teenage boys' bedrooms."

Inside we found Karen and Janeane sitting on Jay's bed supervising and calling encouragement as the men broke through the wall.

They ripped through the last panel, both stopping to wipe sweat from their brow in a mirrored movement.

I crossed my arms, a small grin playing on my lips as I stared at the man who made me feel like a queen.

"I leave you alone for five minutes...."

He shot me a smile, his face covered in a fine layer of white dust. "Sometimes a man sees an opportunity and has to take it."

"It's true," Karrie called from the bed, her fingers busy braiding Janeane's hair. "Will always says he'll get to it but rarely does." She sent me a wink. "The joys of being married to a handyman."

"What can I do to help?"

Jay lifted his shirt to wipe his face, the move revealing yards of his delicious abdomen.

*If I lick him that means I own him, right?*

"Nothing. Sit over there and let the men flex for you."

I started to protest but stopped when Jay leaned in to kiss my forehead.

"I appreciate your offer but I don't want you getting your outfit dirty." He leaned in until his lips were in line with my ear. "I want it in perfect condition for when I tear it from you later."

I sucked in a breath, my hands moving to my push rims. "I'll just be watching over here with the rest of the warrior women."

"Is that us?" Janeane asked.

Karrie laughed, kissing her daughter on the head. "Absolutely."

We watched, commentating and calling out suggestions as the men laboured, Janeane burrowing into the blankets until she finally fell asleep and the men called it a night.

"I think that's our cue," Karen whispered, handing a limp Janeane over to Will. "Lovely to meet you, Frankie."

"You too."

Jay and I waved them off from the porch, his fingers tangled in my hair.

"You know," I said as their truck disappeared from view. "You didn't have to do that."

"I absolutely did."

I tipped my head back, looking up at him. "I was fine using the rec centre."

"Babe, the rec centre closes at eleven and opens at ten."

I cocked an eyebrow. "And?"

"Where are you gonna go after I fuck you at 2 am? Home? Fuck that."

A delicious shiver ran up my spine. "Who said I was staying?"

His fingers tightened in my hair, his body bending, his lips hovering above mine.

"Me."

I licked my lips. "Jay?"

"Mm?"

"I want you to come down my throat."

"Fuck!" His free hand moved to his fly but I brushed it aside.

"No, let me."

Sweaty, dusty, and looking infinitely delicious, Jay fucked my mouth in the shadows of his porch while Harold the raptor watched on.

The taste of him still fresh on my tongue, Jay swept me into his bedroom tying my hands to his bedhead, fucking me until I came again and again and again before his control broke and he came roaring my name.

All in all, a perfect end to a near-perfect night.

## 23

Jay

I lay panting and wrapped around Frankie, the last sizzle of arousal still heating my skin. Her alarm had woken us an hour earlier, and instead of getting out of bed, I'd decided to get into her.

It'd been over a week since I'd knocked down my bathroom wall and Frankie had spent every night in my bed.

"Well, that was—"

"Did that just—?"

We both huffed out tired laughs.

"I think I scratched you," she said, turning her head.

"Like a raptor," I agreed.

"You sound happy about it."

"I am."

Everything felt amazing. Every single part of my life felt fucking perfect.

"God, Jay." Frankie closed her eyes, stretching. "If only I didn't have to go to work."

"Call out. We can stay in bed and make love all day."

She kissed her fingers then pressed them to my mouth. "I'd love to but I have clients. And bills. And I'm pretty sure I need to eat at some point in the near future. Not to mention my shoe collection."

"Ah, yes." I licked her hand, laughing at her squeal. "The near heavenly shoe collection."

"Don't you disparage my babies!"

Her cell rang, the ringtone the one she used to identify clients.

"Shit, give me a second."

I watched a professional mask falling over Frankie's face as she kicked into work mode.

"Hello, this is Frankie."

I rolled out of bed while she spoke to her client giving them privacy. In the kitchen, I made her toast and a large to-go coffee knowing she'd be dashing out the door.

"I'm late!" she cried, scooting through the house, hair in a floppy bun, blouse buttons mismatched, the waistband of her jeggings folded down to reveal a stretch of skin. "Jay, I'm—"

"Late." I laughed. "I know." I held out her thermos of coffee and napkin-wrapped toast. "I'll organise dinner tonight if you need to work late."

She accepted the thermos, dropping the toast in her lap to catch my hand and pull me down for a kiss.

"You're incredible," she whispered against my lips.

I tasted the mint of her toothpaste on her tongue.

"Thank you."

I brushed off her praise. "Least I can do after making you late."

"Mm, worth it." She pressed a last kiss to my lips, then pulled back. "I'll see you—"

Her cell rang again but I didn't recognise the ringtone.

"Who's that?"

"No idea." She handed me back the thermos, answering the call. "Hello, this is Frankie Kenton, how can I help you?"

She listened for a moment, her gaze snapping to me, her eyes growing wider and wider as she stared at me, her mouth forming a little O.

"Yes," she stammered. "I'd absolutely love to. Thank you. Thank you so much."

She hung up, staring at the cell.

"Frankie? You okay?"

Her head slowly rose, her cheeks a pretty pink. "I'm a finalist." She giggled, her hands pressing against her cheeks.

"Rainbow, I don't under—" I stopped, realisation slamming into me. "Shit! The Poddies?"

She nodded. "I'm in the finals. They want me in Cape Hardgrave for the awards. Jay—" She stared up at me, tears glistening on her lashes. "It's happening. It's all happening. They want me to be on panels. They've asked me to be there for the full week. Jay—" She broke off, shaking her head. "I can't believe it."

"I can." I threaded fingers in her hair, peppering her face with kisses. "Proud of you."

"Will you come with me?"

"Of course. Just try to stop me." I kissed her slow and long, tangling our tongues.

"Now." I reached down to cup her breast and give it a playful tweak. "Get to work."

"Fuck! I'm late!"

I handed her the thermos and watched her race for the door.

"Frankie?"

She paused in my entry, her eyes frantic.

The words I love you hovered on the tip of my tongue.

"Jay!" She laughed, hand on the doorknob. "Spit it out!"

I swallowed my feelings. "Have a good day."

She blew me a kiss. "You too!"

I stared into my coffee mug for far too long after she left, trying to figure out what came next.

"The Poddies." I decided. "I'll tell her in Cape Hardgrave over wine, food, and in a bed big enough for eight."

Anxiety hit me, doubts whispering in my ears.

I ran a hand over my beard. "But maybe I'll tie her down first—just in case."

Decision made, I shoved aside the doubts, downed my coffee and began what felt like a good fucking day.

## 24

**Jay**

"When do you leave?" Mai asked, twirling a hotdog over the open fire.

Frankie and I had agreed to cater the Friday night feast after Noah had been called out to a job at the last minute—meaning he'd be late to his own party. With a key to his house and an overabundance of confidence, we'd assured him we had this, but—in a surprise to no one—we'd managed to burn Noah's roast, and been forced to resort to store-bought hotdogs, buns, and brownies.

"Tomorrow," Frankie answered, sending me a grin. "We're road-tripping a day early so we can hit some of the local tourist spots before the festival officially starts on Monday."

"I've heard Cape Hardgrave has one of the best bookstores in the country." Annie licked ketchup from her thumb. "Are you going to check it out?"

"Of course." Frankie released a moan, her head lolling

back dramatically. "I can't wait to see it. I'm gonna buy all the books."

"Jay, fair warning," Noah said from his position on the other side of the fire. "My sister is a book hoarder. You thought the shoes were bad." He shook his head. "She's a lost cause."

I glanced at Frankie cocking an eyebrow. "And where exactly do you keep these books, Dr. Kenton? I haven't seen any evidence of hoarding at your house."

She flushed, glancing down at her fingers mumbling something.

I cupped my ear. "What was that? I didn't catch it."

She cleared her throat. "I store them in Noah's attic. My place doesn't have enough space."

I glanced over at the massive house considering the layout and rapidly calculating possible available space.

"Noah, what are we talking here, man? Is it bad? Do we need to stage an intervention? Is my girl too far gone?"

He grinned, his teeth flashing in the firelight. "A twelve-step program wouldn't go amiss. I couldn't fit a surfboard up there last year."

Frankie snatched up a marshmallow tossing it at her brother. "Liar!"

"Fine, it's only like ninety-nine-point-nine-nine percent Frankie's shit."

"That's it," she declared, crossing her arms over her chest, nose in the air. "You're dead to me. I disown you." She twisted, glaring at me. "And if you think you're getting lucky tonight you can think again."

I chuckled, leaning over to hook an arm around her neck, pulling her close to playfully smooch her cheek. "You're adorable when you're feisty."

"Frankie, do you have many meetings lined up for this

week?" Flo asked, from her spot next to Ren, both of them picking from a plate of brownies balanced on his knee.

"A few."

I shuffled my chair closer to Frankie, keeping my arm draped around her shoulders.

"Who with?" Annie asked, her back stubbornly to Linc who sat on the opposite side of the fire pit.

"Green Media, Ross and Co Broadcasting, and SuperNick."

"Are you thinking of selling the podcast?" Linc asked, slowly rotating his hotdog over the fire.

"Never. Babe, hit me."

I chuckled, handing her two marshmallows.

"I want to move into television," she continued, threading the marshmallows on her stick. "I'd love to try my hand at a talk show or documentary, but I'd be open to a guest spot. Anything really."

"I know it's your dream but I can't imagine anything worse than being on TV." Mai shuddered. "Even the podcast feels like an invasion of privacy."

"That's because you're a hardcore introvert." Flo licked chocolate from her fingers. "You'd be happy living in a cabin in the woods if we let you."

"It's true. Can you make that happen?"

"Does that mean you'll have to move?" Ren asked, pulling the conversation back to Frankie.

"Maybe."

I flinched, my arm tensing around her.

The conversation moved on but I got stuck on her comment. I shifted closer, dropping my voice to keep our conversation between us.

"Move?" I asked. "You never mentioned moving?"

Frankie raised one shoulder in a half shrug watching her

bubbling marshmallows. "There's nothing to say. Everything is subject to an offer and I can tell you I certainly don't have one of those." She glanced over, a little smile playing on her lips. "I started down this track before you, but now my priorities seem to be changing."

"What's that mean?"

"You're definitely a consideration."

My chest tightened, a heavy weight settling on my shoulders. "You're not fucking changing your dream for me."

She blinked. "Why not?"

"I'm not worth it."

She snorted, her hand snaking up to cup my neck. "Okay, I'm gonna need you to stop speaking about yourself that way. You're important to me, and I'm loving what we're building together. Until something eventuates there's nothing to discuss. But if something does happen, we'll talk and work it out together." She wiggled her eyebrows suggestively. "But if you want to send me a dick pic as practice for a potential future long-distance relationship, I won't say no."

The tightness in my chest didn't release but I ignored it, focusing on Frankie. "With or without erection? 'Cause I could—"

She laughed, pulling me down for a kiss. "You're terrible."

"But you like me."

"Mm, I do."

Her tongue licked at my lips, my mouth parting to allow her entrance, our tongues tangling. I shifted, changing our angle, deepening our kiss, relishing her hot little moan—a bolt of lust rocketing straight to my cock. The tension in my chest melted away leaving need in its place.

"Ew!" Annie threw a wadded-up napkin our way. "Get a room!"

I took my time ending the kiss, my teeth gently catching her bottom lip before letting her go. "That's a good suggestion. Shall we?"

Frankie laughed, tossing her stick into the fire. "I thought you weren't getting lucky tonight."

"That's fine." I tangled my fingers in her hair, pressing our foreheads together. "I'll concentrate on you. On your body, on your reactions, on your sweet clit."

She shivered, her eyes flashing. "You're evil."

"And you're adorable."

"Take me to bed, Jay."

"With pleasure."

## 25

Frankie

"Wow, this is incredible." I pushed into the bungalow, taking in the rich furnishings and amazing view.

The Poddie people had put us up at Cape Hardgrave's Four Seasons. I'd asked for an accessible room but when we'd arrived at check-in, we'd discovered the studio room in the main building had been double-booked. With no other accessible rooms available in the main hotel, the concierge had upgraded us to an accessible oceanfront bungalow—apologising profusely for the inconvenience.

"Oh my God," I squealed, staring at the bed. "Ten people could fit on there."

"Babe, any time you get an upgrade, call me." Jay dropped our luggage in the middle of the room. "It has its own kitchen."

"Kitchen? Look at the view!" I moved through the space, turning in a circle to survey the suite. "I can assure you this has never, *ever* happened to me before."

Jay took a flying leap to land on the bed with a heavy flop.

"Oh fuck. It's so fucking good." He squirmed around, making a mess of the bed covers. "This mattress is incredible."

I laughed, heading for the bathroom. "I'll come lie on it in a minute. My bladder is about to burst. Remind me of this moment the next time I think a supersize slushie is a good idea."

"Road trips are made for junk food," Jay called through the bathroom door. "It's practically a requirement."

"I'm going to be peeing purple for days."

"Nawww, even your pee will be rainbow-coloured."

I heard him moving around while I finished washing up.

"What are you doing out there?"

"Nothing."

I pulled the door open, finding Jay with his head buried in a closet.

"Mm, it certainly looks like nothing."

He jerked back, shooting me a boyish grin. "I'm just looking. Don't ruin my fun."

"Looking for what?"

He lifted one shoulder in a half-shrug. "I'll know it when I see it."

"That shouldn't be profound and yet it is."

Jay abandoned the closet, snatching my hand to pull me across to the water view. He moved to hug me from behind, his chin dropping to my shoulder.

"This is a good day," he whispered, kissing my temple.

"No," I corrected softly. "This is a best day."

I turned my head, losing myself in his eyes.

*I love you.* The words hovered unspoken between us, courage failing me.

"Say it," he whispered, his lips close enough to brush mine. "Say what you're thinking."

I swallowed, trembling. "I can't."

"Then let me." His mouth grazed my lips. "I love you, Frankie."

I melted, leaning into his kiss, letting him taste everything I wanted to say.

"I love you too," I whispered, leaning my forehead against his. "You're an easy man to love, Jay. Very easy."

*Be brave. Take a chance.*

Banishing any doubts from my mind, I reached for him, brushing fingers across his cheekbones and down his neck.

"Jay?"

"Mm?"

"Make love to me."

He stepped back. "I thought you'd never ask."

I moved to the bed, my gaze locked on Jay's beautiful body as I transitioned.

*He's so fucking beautiful.*

He ducked into the bathroom and I could hear the tap running as he washed his hands, a deep aching beginning at the sound. If I wasn't careful, I'd develop a Pavlovian response to running water and wouldn't that be awkward?

Jay walked back into the suite, his biceps flexing as he peeled his shirt off revealing deliciously sculpted abdominal muscles.

I shifted on the bed, ready and wanting him.

"You're still wearing clothing." His statement had me reaching for my top.

"And you're still wearing pants."

His grin looked like pure sin. "Not for long."

He kicked off his shoes, hands sliding down his body to slowly unbuckle his belt.

*Why is he so hot? It's unnatural.*

"Hurry up, rainbow."

Jay's tease felt like a caress against my skin, my nipples hardening in the cups of my bra.

I pulled my shirt off, tossing it on the growing pile of discarded clothes.

Gazes locked, we both began to slide pants and underwear down our legs, my teeth sinking into my bottom lip when his cock bounced free.

Heavy, thick and perfectly rigid, I wanted to lick him from root to crown, savouring the salt of his skin.

Naked, Jay sauntered across the room, his body moving with the preternatural grace of a predator stalking its prey.

I reached behind me, unhooking my bra to slip it down my arms, dangling the lace-covered piece from my fingertip.

"Fuck, you're beautiful."

His head dipped, tongue swirling over my left areola while his thumb glided over my right.

"You're a monster," I whispered, grazing fingernails over his back.

"Really?" He lifted up. "'Cause I can stop."

I cupped my breasts, offering them to him like some kind of debauched goddess. "Can you?"

He groaned, dropping back to nuzzle at the valley between them. "No, absolutely not."

I burned to make Jay feel even half the love and need I did. I wanted to make him ache with pleasure, to hear him swear against my lips as we both came.

I pressed him back, urging him to lie down beside me.

"My turn."

I kissed the space above his heart then shifted, repositioning my legs until I could bend over his body, working my way down. I skated tiny kisses across his abdomen, my tongue delving and dipping, licking until Jay became a panting wreck under my mouth.

"Suck me."

His groaned order intensified the throbbing ache in my core. I reached down to touch myself, raising my hand to press my soaked fingers to his mouth. He muttered a curse, sucking my fingers clean.

I bent, my mouth closing around him, sucking him deep.

"Fuck!"

I deep-throated Jay, loving the feel of him on my tongue, the weight of his balls in my hand, the taste of him.

"Fuck," he groaned again, his hips arching up. "Fuck, fuck, fuck!"

Jay jackknifed up, ripping me from his cock.

"What are you—?"

"I need to be in you. I need to feel you around me."

I placed a hand on his chest, halting his movement. "If you want that, then let me ride you."

He blinked. "You want to?"

" Oh, yeah." I gestured at the low headboard. "And that's perfect."

In a tangle of limbs, kisses and laughter, we got into position, Jay's hands on my ass, my right hand braced beside his shoulder, my left gripping the headboard.

He rolled on the condom, pressing a kiss to the underside of my breast.

"Ready?" he asked, nipping at my lips.

"Fuck yes."

He guided himself into me and I shifted using my arms to ease onto his cock.

"Fuck," he swore, head falling back against the pillow. "You feel fucking incredible."

I made a sound in the back of my throat, his cock

stretching me. With tentative movements I began to rock, my arms and core working overtime to move my body up his shaft, the glide of him delicious. Jay's hands supported my ass, helping me set a rhythm.

"That's it," Jay praised. "Fuck my cock, rainbow. Fuck me. Let me stretch you out. Feels good, doesn't it? My big cock fucking your tight pussy."

He crunched up, shifting my hand to his shoulder, his hand sliding between us to find my clit, pinching and rubbing as I rode his dick.

"Come for me, rainbow. Come around my dick. Fuck me, baby. Let me feel that hot squeeze as you milk me."

I whimpered, ruined by his filthy words, destroyed by him.

"Fuck, Jay, I'm going to—" I arched, teetering on the edge of a glorious rush.

"No, you don't."

Jay stopped, pulling back, grinning at my whimper of protest.

"What are you doing? Come back."

He held me in place, the tip of one finger rubbing circles around my clit.

"More," I demanded. "Jay, I need more."

He eased his cock out then back in, the glide simultaneously too much and not enough.

"Jay, please."

He thrust up, fucking into me, his cock branding me from the inside.

"I love you," I cried, my body shattering. "I fucking love you."

Clenching and bowing, my arms rocking me, I milked his cock, fucking him deep into me.

"Frankie!" Jay's control broke, his teeth nipping at my

shoulder, sucking the bite away.

We slowed, panting together in the aftermath. I tried to move away but he halted me, muttering a small protest.

"Stay, just for a minute."

And so we remained, joined together, our bodies slowly cooling.

"Did you mean it?" I asked, my voice barely a whisper.

"Mean what?" Jay asked, his fingers stroking lazily through my hair.

"That you love me?"

He cupped my cheek, searching my gaze. "Yes. You're incredible, Frankie. I'd be a fool not to love you."

Our mouths melded together, our kiss deepening.

"Again?" I asked against his mouth.

"You have to ask?"

With a squealed laugh he fell back against the bed, taking me down with him—and kept me there.

## 26

**Jay**

I straightened my tie in the hall mirror, giving myself a once-over.

*Not bad for a kid from the Cove.*

"And you're sure," I asked Frankie, turning away from the mirror. "This is a fancy dinner?"

Frankie's laugh carried from the bathroom. "For the millionth time, yes! Tonight's the formal announcement of the nominees and the welcome dinner. The festival starts tomorrow and there's the awards gala next Saturday."

"You want a drink?" I asked, pulling a beer from the mini-fridge.

"No, I'm okay. Can you read out the other nominees though? I want to see if I can remember their names and subjects."

I sat at the table cracking a beer to take a pull as I flicked through the papers Chrissy had dropped off at lunch.

"Damn it," I heard Frankie mutter. "I did get sunburnt."

"Worth it."

"For you, maybe. You got to perve on my breasts while all I got was sunburn."

"And sex."

She laughed. "True. The sex was great."

"Need me to kiss them better?"

"Later. For now, I'm going to smother them in concealer and hope no one notices."

I laughed, turning back to the papers, sorting through the descriptions of the other nominees and their respective podcasts.

I picked one at random, snorting as I read the description.

"Well, this one's not gonna win." I tossed it on the table. "Who cares about frogs?"

Frankie laughed. "Lots of people. It's a popular podcast."

"And this one?" I held up the paper, putting on an old-timey accent. "An introspection on the lives and loves of the characters of *The Junction*." I dropped the paper frowning at the ocean view. "What the fuck is *The Junction*?"

"A 1950s TV show, apparently." Frankie poked her head around the bathroom door, half her hair in beach curls, the other still straight. "It made a comeback last year thanks to a streaming service."

"Yep, definitely not in the top three."

"Jay!"

"What? You want me to lie?"

She chuckled, shaking her head. "You're incorrigible."

"And you're going to be late."

She ducked back in, scooting her chair back to the vanity. "There are some I'm really worried about."

"Like?"

"*Misadventures of a Mistress*."

"As in she's a mistress?"

"Read the packet."

I searched through the papers, locating it toward the bottom of the pile.

"Found it." I straightened the paper with a dramatic flourish, clearing my throat to begin reading.

"*Misadventures of a Mistress* is a storytelling masterpiece exploring one woman's sexual progress from divorcee to divine goddess. Are you ready to take the plunge? Featuring real stories from McKenzie Rylan's—" I coughed, choking on her name.

"You okay?" Frankie called. "Need some water?"

I cleared my throat. "I'm fine." I stared at the description, feeling like I'd taken a hit to the solar plexus.

*Shit. Shit. Shit. Shit. Shit. Shit.*

I swallowed, a cesspit of anxiety crawling in my stomach. "Do you know McKenzie?"

"Who? Oh, Rylan? No. Well, kind of. I know *of* her. She's got a large following but her podcast isn't my thing. I think she changes the name of the people she talks about but it still feels a little voyeuristic to me."

I scanned the list of episodes she'd been judged on, my gaze snagging one entitled, "The First Boy Toy Part 1"— reportedly her most popular episode.

"Chrissy wanted to sign her for a while but said something about red flags. Anyway, you'll be able to meet her tonight. I think she's at our table."

Sweat broke out on my brow, my chest feeling like it had been gripped by a vice, the pressure mounting.

"Babe?" I called, my voice hoarse.

"Mm?"

"I... I gotta get something from the car. You gonna be long?"

"About twenty minutes? We don't have to be at dinner

for another half hour though." She wheeled back, poking her head out the doorway, a curler in one hand. "But I wanted to mingle at pre-drinks." She frowned. "You okay? You look pale."

"Fine." I surged to my feet, searching for her car keys. "Just need to—to make a call. I'll be back."

"Jay. Where are you—"

I slammed the bungalow door, cutting Frankie off and hurried for the parking lot. Heart in my throat I pounded down the walkway, keys digging into my palm.

*Fuck, fuck, fuck, fuck.*

In the car, I connected my cell, navigating to McKenzie's 'Boy Toy' episode, dread building.

"Jesus Jay, what the fuck are you doing?" I muttered.

A call popped on my screen, Frankie's name appearing. I sent her to voicemail, too emotionally fucked up to speak to her.

"Fuck it. Just get it over with."

I slid my thumb across the screen, dragging the play bar to around the ten-minute mark and hit play.

"—he loved to please." McKenzie's voice filled the car, my stomach clenching in response. "Overeager. Delightfully so. The boy had a mouth on him that didn't know when to quit. I taught him everything I knew. Which led to our eventual downfall. He fell in love with me." She laughed, her voice overly loud in the car.

"Can't say I blame him," McKenzie's guest host quipped. "You're an incredible woman."

"Oh, I know." She chuckled, the sound raising the hairs on the back of my neck. "But you have to understand, John. This boy didn't just *love* me. He wanted to *marry* me. He whisked me away to Mexico, spending a fortune on a romantic weekend. I, of course, had no idea of his intentions. While he sat at dinner waiting for me to arrive, I was fucking the bellboy in our hotel room."

Her guest burst out laughing, making a fucking mockery of one of the worst moments of my fucking life.

I ran my finger along the play bar, randomly stopping again.

"So you're telling me," the guest host said, laughter in his voice. "After all that, this kid thought you'd settle down and be his old lady?"

McKenzie laughed. "He did! And I had to be the one to break it to him—he'd never be anything but a good lay. A guy like him wasn't made for relationships."

Their laughter rang in my ears as the memories of that night assaulted me. Waiting for hours at the restaurant, the wait staff exchanging pitying glances while hope died a cruel death. Finally going in search of McKenzie, worried she'd been hurt only to find her passed out beside the bellboy in the bed I'd paid for.

I'd thrown the fucker out and we'd spent hours arguing, McKenzie crying and wailing, turning it around on me.

"You're good for sex but we both know you're not someone you marry. You're not built for relationships." She'd cupped my cheek, tears glistening on her eyelashes. "The sooner you reconcile that this is who you are, the better."

I hadn't believed her. Hadn't wanted to believe her. But then my next girlfriend had said the same thing, and the next, and I'd been forced to face the truth—I was the fuck boy, not the forever guy.

I scrubbed a hand over my face, swearing under my breath.

My cell chimed with a message from Frankie.

FRANKIE

Jay, are you alright? Where are you? You're
worrying me.

I stared at her message, my stomach rolling, a weird acid taste on my tongue.

A second message followed suit.

FRANKIE

If this is about the sunburn, I forgive you.
Just come back. Please.

Some of my tension eased, my shoulders relaxing.

"She doesn't need to know about McKenzie. It's history. I'm not that guy anymore."

I looked down at my cell, the lock screen image a selfie of Frankie and I on her couch, both of us wearing face masks with towels wrapped around our heads, laughing.

My tension eased, my body relaxing.

"I'm not that fucking guy."

I sucked in a deep breath, swiping to my gallery, scrolling through pictures of Frankie.

"Pull your shit together," I ordered. "McKenzie's opinion doesn't mean shit. She's the past. Frankie's your future."

With renewed focus, I climbed out of Frankie's car, determined to make this night about the one person who mattered—Frankie.

## 27

**Frankie**

Something was wrong. Jay had been quiet all through the cocktail hour, his expression polite but distant. Anyone who didn't know him would see him as quiet, charming and interested. But I saw through his mask.

"Are you sure you're alright?" I asked, placing a hand on his arm. "Did you get too much sun? I can handle dinner by myself if you need to go lie down."

Jay shook his head. "I'm fine." He dropped a kiss on my forehead. "Don't worry, I wouldn't miss this, Frankie."

I nearly believed him. I nearly discarded all my concerns and gave myself over to having a good night.

But I didn't because one look into his flat green eyes and I knew—everything was *not* fine.

"Looks like they're going in. Shall we?" Jay asked, sweeping an arm toward the now open banquet room.

I nodded, glancing up at him as he walked beside me looking as if he were headed to a torture chamber.

I didn't know what had happened to make him walk out of our hotel room but I was determined to figure it out.

"Which table?" he asked, looking around the lavish hall.

"Table three." I lifted my arm pointing across the room. "That's us."

We found our places, Jay settling in beside me.

"This is nice."

I nodded, pursing my lips. "Jay." I waited for him to meet my gaze before continuing. "What's going on?"

He glanced away. "Nothing. It's... nothing. Well, not nothing, it's just something I gotta work through."

Nervous anxiety began to churn in my stomach. I slipped my hands under the table to rub sweaty palms against the skirt of my dress. "You're worrying me. Should we go? We can head back to the bungalow and talk."

For a second, he looked like he'd agree. I watched a cacophony of emotions play across his face, his eyes closing. "Frankie, there's something I need to tell you."

I reached out, linking my fingers with his. "Okay. Let's go somewhere quiet. We can—"

"Jay? Well, isn't this a surprise? It's been a long time."

Jay froze, his face blank.

I twisted, looking over the table to see a stunning woman staring at Jay with the same expression I assumed a piranha wore before it attacked.

My back stiffened, warning sirens wailing in my ears.

"Well?" the woman prompted as she slid gracefully into the seat across the table. "Aren't you going to introduce me to your... friend?"

I sucked in a breath at her deliberate pause, swiftly recognising that this wasn't a woman I wanted anything to do with.

In my profession, I met hundreds of people from clients

to family members to hospital staff. I'd become an expert at picking out personality traits and assessing people with one glance. I trusted my experience and my intuition, and both said to stay away.

"I'm Doctor Frankie Kenton," I said, giving her a nod. "I don't think we've been introduced. You are?"

"McKenzie Rylan." She knit her fingers together, her gaze trained on Jay. "I didn't expect to see you here."

Jay cleared his throat. "I didn't expect to see you either."

I glanced at Jay, confused by his reaction to her.

*Is she a former lover? Someone in the kink scene? Did they sleep together? Is there something else going on?*

Questions burned in my throat but I swallowed them, recognising that he needed my support. My explanations could wait.

She gave him a once-over that rubbed me the wrong way, the hairs on my arms standing at attention. My hand snaked out to find his under the table, squeezing tight.

On the surface, McKenzie looked to be in her mid-to-late-forties, but the fine lines at the corners of her mouth and eyes hinted that she could be older. From the top of her perfectly coiffed blonde hair to the bottom of her fire-red figure-hugging dress, the woman looked like a supermodel —glorious and glamorous in a way that suggested she'd be beautiful even at ninety.

But like Snow White's apple, I suspected the skin hid a poisoned core.

Finished with her perusal, I watched her lips curl into an approving smile. "It's good to see you, Jay. You always did scrub up well."

Something sinister hatched in my belly, the fine hairs on the back of my neck prickling.

"McKenzie!" A group of people surrounded our table, pulling her attention from Jay.

I leaned in, my lips hovering close to his ear. "Who is she to you?"

He turned slightly, his expression unreadable. "She's the cougar I told you about."

I relaxed slightly. "So, she's an ex. Awkward but no biggie."

"She's also the woman I found cheating on me."

I winced.

"On the night I'd planned to propose to her."

*Fuck. Fuckity, fuck, fuck, fuck!*

A million thoughts raced through my head—none of them good.

"Are you over her?"

He scoffed. "Fuck yes."

My stomach unclenched. "Alright. So, there's no problem here?"

He glanced at McKenzie. "Nothing except that she's an unwelcome intrusion in our romantic week away."

I saw a spark of my Jay return. "Should I call Harold and see if he's willing to take her out? A raptor loose in the banquet hall seems like the perfect solution to this situation."

Jay chuckled, his big hand squeezing mine. "Thank you. I needed that."

I leaned in to kiss his smiling mouth. "Don't mention it. When you meet my ex, you can do the same."

Jay's face dropped, his eyes glinting in a way that chased away all the negative feelings, leaving a flush of heat in its wake.

"Why the fuck would I be meeting your ex?"

I patted him on the knee. "Don't worry, he's a nice guy. We still catch up for coffee when he's in town."

"I am not emotionally mature enough for this conversation."

I laughed. "Go get us some drinks. You can brood later."

"Brood?" He leaned in, one hand cupping my neck to bring me closer to him. "I'm gonna fuck you until I'm the only man you remember."

Liquid fire lit in my core.

"Go before I drag you under the table," I ordered.

With a wink, Jay sat back, his hand slow to let go. "Love you, Frankie."

"Love you too."

He stood then paused, leaning down.

"I'm sorry for not telling you. She's my past and it fucked me up at the time." His thumb grazed my bottom lip. "But you're my future. I didn't want her to touch what we have."

My insides turned into a warm gooey mess.

"You're forgiven."

He grinned. "You should have made me grovel."

"Oh, I will. In bed. Later. Those ropes? They're going to be for you."

He barked out a laugh. "You wish."

I watched him walk to the bar silently appreciating the cup of his bottom in those pants.

"I didn't realise you two were together."

My shoulders snapped back, my head twisting to look at McKenzie. She watched me, one hand swirling her wine glass.

"Are you enjoying your night?" I asked, determined to change the subject.

"Not particularly." She lifted a one-shouldered shrug. "These dinners are normally such a bore."

I always gave people the benefit of the doubt. I firmly believed given enough time, effort, and support, people could change. We were all capable of growth.

Annie hated my theory and regularly tried to convince me otherwise. Up until this moment, I'd never been tempted to reject my ideals, just worked extra hard to find a middle ground with people.

But now? Now I wanted to tell McKenzie where she could shove her judgment.

*Deep breaths, Frankie. Don't let your jealousy and protectiveness of Jay get muddled. She might be a nice woman. She might be nervous and awkward like Mai gets sometimes.*

"Have you been to many?" I asked politely.

She downed her wine and stood, smoothing down her skirt. "Enough."

And with that she walked away, leaving me to question younger Jay's taste in women.

"Oh," I muttered, watching her stroll toward the bar. "He is *so* getting shit about this later."

## 28

Jay

"A double scotch, a mojito, and a coke, thanks." I pushed some cash in the tip jar, leaning on the makeshift bar.

"She's cute."

My back straightened, body tensing as McKenzie slid in beside me.

"What are you doing here, McKenzie?"

She leaned a hip against the bar, watching the crowd as they moved around, finding their seats.

"I could ask you the same question but your little friend made it rather obvious." She leaned over, resting a hand on my arm. "I have to say, I'm surprised by you."

I shifted, moving away from her cloying perfume and possessive touch. I didn't care if it was fucking rude, I didn't want to be in her presence a moment longer than necessary.

While the emotions of that fucking night had long since faded, the detritus of my life took longer to heal. She'd destroyed me. Destroyed the concept of who I was and what

I wanted in life. For fucking years I'd convinced myself I wasn't anything better than disposable.

But not now. Not with Frankie.

"You know, I'm curious," she said, her tone light.

I watched the bartender mix Frankie's cocktail, determined to ignore her.

"You seem to like her and yet you've allowed her to become attached." McKenzie paused and I could feel the weight of her gaze on me. "Do you really expect her to fall in love with you?"

My hands curled into fists, my stomach churning.

"You're a fuck boy, Jay. You know that. You're not built for relationships."

*Fuck.*

"Which is why I have to ask, why are you leading that poor girl on when you know it will end in heartache?"

The bartender slid the drinks across the counter, turning to McKenzie.

"What can I get you?"

She glanced at my order, a small smile pulling at her cherry red lips. "I'll take a double scotch."

I stared at the liquid in the small tumbler, the taste of it souring for me.

"Here." I shoved it across the wood countertop. "Take this one, I've lost my taste for it."

I picked up our remaining drinks and headed back to the table, my stomach rolling as a cold sweat dampened my back.

"Jay?"

I paused, glancing over my shoulder at her.

"You know I'm only telling the truth. It's nothing personal."

I gritted my teeth. "Just like it wasn't personal the night

you fucked a bellboy in our room?"

Around us the chatter of the crowd died, turning to stare.

"Have a good night, McKenzie." I nodded at the glass in her hand. "Enjoy your drink."

I turned away, forcing myself to take slow, measured steps back to Frankie.

*You're a fuck boy, Jay. You know that.*

Her poisonous words began to creep under my skin, cutting through flesh and bone like arrows to tear holes in my walls.

I forced a smile on my face, determined to focus on the only person who mattered—Frankie.

I wove through the crowd, noting most of the tables were now occupied, attendees getting ready for the dinner to begin.

At our table, Frankie accepted my offered cocktail with a laugh. "I didn't realise we were undertaking Operation Get-Frankie-Drunk." She took a pull on her straw, her lips smacking with satisfaction. "Mm, that's good."

I forced myself to relax, dropping into my seat. "What's the plan for tonight?"

Frankie handed me a small printed card with the night's menu on one side and the order of ceremony on the other.

*God damn it.*

"McKenzie's the keynote speaker," I muttered, tossing the card on the table.

"You want to talk about her or about the possibility of anal later?"

I coughed, my head whipping around to stare at Frankie. She sent me a wink.

"That got your attention."

My hand slid under the table, cruising up her leg until I

found a sensitive spot on her thigh.

"Jay!" she hissed, leaning into me. "What are you doing?"

"Finding a warm place for my hand." I nuzzled her neck. "It's cold, rainbow."

She lightly slapped my hand, laughing when I nipped her earlobe. "Stop it! You can play later."

"Or I can play now." I lowered my voice, mindful of the other people seated at the table. "I saw a bathroom we could—"

"Absolutely not." Frankie shook her head. "Bathrooms are disgusting." She bit her lip, her expression sultry. "But I saw a cloakroom earlier."

"Fuck you're perfect for me."

I kissed her, ignoring the room around us, determined to enjoy an evening with my woman celebrating her accomplishments.

The music began to drop, the conversation around us slowing. The lights in the room dimmed, leaving the stage illuminated.

"Welcome to the Poddie's Festival. I'm your host, Gareth. Let's get this party started!"

The MC kicked off the night with terrible jokes and a song that lasted for far too long. Frankie and I exchanged amused looks, our lips pressed together to keep from laughing.

"And now, I'm excited to invite our keynote speaker for this evening to the stage—Ms. McKenzie Rylan."

I'd managed to avoid looking across the table, focusing on Frankie, the stage, and my meal. But as the crowd applauded and McKenzie made her way up to the stage accepting shakes and smiling brilliantly, I found myself unable to look away.

This feels like a car crash in slow motion.

"Thank you for having me." Her gaze swept across the crowded room, her expression light and friendly.

"I thought I'd give an overview of how I came to be in this room with your beautiful selves," she began, raising her left hand. "As you can see, no ring. But for nearly seventeen years I wore one, raised a kid, settled for being a dutiful housewife." She focused on me, a small smile playing on her lips. "Until my husband left and I met the first boy toy."

Around the room a few people hooted, calling out explicit suggestions.

"You always remember your first, and that young man gave me many firsts. First orgasm via oral, first public sex act, first time I cheated on someone." She lifted one shoulder in a self-deprecating manner. "Oops. We all make mistakes. And as you know, I make more than my fair share."

Instead of being upset, the room played to her joke, laughing with her.

*Laughing at the ruins of my life.*

The emotions I'd thought long buried rose like zombies, their rotting corpses septic shots to my soul.

"Well, in true Mistress fashion, I have a little surprise for the group." She stared directly at me. "He's here tonight."

Frankie's hand snaked out, gripping mine. I looked at her, finding her face flushed, her gaze locked on McKenzie.

"Jay Wood, everybody! The original boy toy. Let's give him a round of applause."

I watched the colour drain from Frankie's face. I watched her head slowly turn to me. I watched her gaze meet mine, seeing the horror reflected in her eyes.

I surged to my feet, starting for the doors of the hall, determined to get the fuck out of here before I did anything further to hurt the woman I loved.

"And there he goes. Always running from commitment," McKenzie taunted me from the stage, the crowd laughing as if this were some kind of joke.

"Fuck," I swore, shoving through the banquet doors. "Fuck, fuck, fuck!"

"Jay! Jay, wait! Jay!"

I stopped in the reception area, turning to see Frankie frantically wheeling toward me.

"Frankie, go back to your dinner."

"No." She coasted to a stop in front of me, arms crossing over her chest. "Absolutely not. We're talking this out."

*The fuck we were.*

"Please, Frankie. Go back inside."

"No. That was disgusting. I cannot believe she—"

"Said the truth? Told the world what I am? What I'll always be?" I laughed darkly, my heart hurting.

"How can you say that?" Frankie asked, staring at me with her big blue eyes. "How can you even think that's who you are?"

I looked into her eyes and finally admitted the truth.

"I can't do this." I ran a hand through my hair, pulling at the ends. "This is too hard, Frankie. It's not working."

"That's a fucking lie. You love me."

"Sometimes love isn't enough."

She reeled back as if I'd slapped her—and my heart began to fracture.

"You don't mean it."

I turned away from her, pulling on my tie to loosen the material from around my neck.

Silence stretched between us.

"Don't do something you'll regret," she whispered. "Please talk to me."

For the briefest moment, I wavered. I half turned toward her, a yearning ache in my gut.

But seeing the raw hope on her face hardened my resolve. If she thought tonight was bad, a lifetime with me would be hell. Better to end things before they became too serious.

"It's over, Frankie."

"It's not!"

"Don't make this harder than it is."

"Make it harder?" she choked. "Make what harder? Destroying a relationship because of a vindictive ex? You're not the man she says you are. You're incredible, Jay. You're loyal, and trustworthy, and you make me so fucking happy."

Tears slid down her cheeks, my fingers aching to brush them away.

"Don't do this," she whispered, her voice catching. "Please don't do this."

I stared at her, my gaze trailing up and down her body, memorising every curve and plane, every colour and shadow.

"Goodbye, Frankie."

"Jay, wait. Jay!"

I turned on my heel, heading for the door.

"Jay!"

I could hear her wheeling behind me, her voice heavy with tears.

"Fucking hell, Jay! Stop! Talk to me."

There wasn't anything left to say. Relationships weren't my strong suit, and trying to convince myself otherwise would only end in heartache.

I left, not looking back, not listening, determined to let her go despite my aching heart.

*Fuck, it hurt like hell.*

**Frankie**

He'd gone. The fucking bastard had packed up his shit and left. By the time I'd gotten to the bungalow he'd left. The only trace of him were my car keys and a wad of cash on the bed—as if this were a scene from fucking *Pretty Woman* or something.

I'd tapped out a text because even as my heart broke, I needed to know he was okay.

FRANKIE

> Text me when you're somewhere safe. I don't need to speak to you, I don't need an apology or an explanation. I just need to know you're safe.

His response had come through an hour ago.

JAY

> I'm safe.

> And I'm sorry.

That had been it—five little words that said everything and nothing.

"He's a fuckwit," Annie raged down the phone line. "He white-fanged you. What a fucking idiot! I'll kill him. I'll goddamn kill him!"

"It's okay," I whispered, my voice thick with tears. "He's hurting too. We'll figure it out."

"I don't know," Mai said slowly, her voice almost cautious. "I don't know if we want you figuring this out. It shouldn't be up to you to heal this man, Frankie. He needs to do that himself."

I waited for Flo to chime in with her usual positivity but found the line silent.

"Flo? What are you thinking?"

A sigh met my question. "There's so much to unpack. His first love, the woman he thought he'd marry, hurting him so badly he convinced himself he couldn't have meaningful relationships. The return of the vindictive ex just as he's found new love and is beginning to trust himself." She blew out another long breath. "It's got all the hallmarks of a tragic but wonderful love story."

"Except this isn't a love story," Annie burst in. "This is Frankie's life. And the frog turned into a toad instead of a prince."

"But all things are darkest before dawn," Flo said, her voice low and soothing. "What do you want, Frankie? What does your heart, your gut, and your mind say?"

I closed my eyes, tears leaking down my cheeks. "That he had a knee-jerk reaction and I should give him space. That this isn't about me—it's about Jay's past and unresolved issues from terrible past relationships." I choked my throat closing. "I want to go to him. I want to help him work this out but I'm scared and he's scared, and this is a big fucking mess and I can't. I have to be here. I have a panel tomorrow, and meetings and—" I broke off, words failing.

"Let go," Mai encouraged. "It's okay, babe. Let it out."

I ranted, cursing out McKenzie, cursing out Jay, my heart feeling as if it had been broken into a million pieces.

After, I lay spent on the bed, my eyes closed, the tears all cried out.

"Go to sleep, Frankie," Flo whispered as I began to drift off. "Things will be better in the morning."

I hit end on the call, and rolled onto my back, giving in to the numbness of sleep.

I WOKE to a loud pounding on my door. I blinked, my eyes feeling like sandpaper, brushing limp hair from my face.

"Fuck," I muttered, groaning as I sat up. "Fuck me."

I moved to my wheelchair, dropping my phone in my lap, briefly wondering if I'd missed a fire alarm.

I yanked the door open, my hand shooting out to prevent Chrissy from falling into me.

"What the fuck, Christine? What's wrong?"

"You did it!" she screeched, grabbing my hand and jumping up and down. "They want you in New York. They want you in New York!"

My breath caught. "Who wants me in New York?"

"Green Media." She pushed me back, slamming the door and running across the room to raid the mini bar. "Babe, we were wrong. They don't want to meet today—they want to talk contracts today. They want a pilot. They want you —bad."

I closed my eyes, gratitude and excitement mixed with my heartache to create a bittersweet brew.

"This is amazing news," I told her, sucking back tears. "Absolutely brilliant."

"Wait." She stood, staring at me. "What's wrong? Why don't you sound excited?" She glanced around. "And where the fuck is Jay?"

My voice cracked. "He tried to break up with me last night."

"Tried?"

I huffed out a laugh. "I'm stubborn. He's hurting and dealt with it the only way he knew how—which was to try and protect the person he loved from himself."

"Oh, babe." She crossed the room to wrap me in a tight hug. "Stupid question, but are you alright?"

"No," I admitted, swiping at my wet cheeks. "I'm absolutely gutted. I wanted him to choose me, Chrissy. I wanted him to be strong enough to ignore all the doubt and fear that was within him even though I know there's nothing more powerful in the world. Even though I've worked with people thousands of times who have done the same thing I'm just so...." I trailed off.

She pulled back, crouching in front of me. "So?" she prompted quietly.

"Angry. Hurt. Disappointed. Anxious. Conflicted." I sucked in a shaky breath. "And in love. So fucking in love with him I ache that he's not here."

"Ah."

I waited, frowning when she didn't expand.

"Ah? Ah? That's it? That's all you're going to say?"

"Babe." She grinned. "You're a fucking psychologist. What more do you need me to say?"

I blew out a breath. "You're right. Though I'll admit it's a shit ton harder to be distant and objective when you're the one going through the emotions."

"Save it for an episode," she joked. "But seriously, Frankie." She squeezed my hand. "I'm here for you."

"I know. Thank you." I wiped at my cheeks. "Now go away so I can get ready."

"I'm not gonna—" Her phone beeped. "Fuck. Fine." She waggled a finger at me. "I'm going but I'll see you at lunch where we'll talk strategy over midday mimosas."

I nodded, waving her off. "Go! I need a shower."

Chrissy walked to the door, pausing in the entry. "And babe? Congratulations. I'm sending you their offer right now" She held up her phone. "We're gonna make them beg at this meeting."

I huffed out a laugh. "I'll see you at lunch."

She left and I sat for a moment watching the waves crash against the shore.

As much as I ached to follow Jay, I had responsibilities here. I'd sold tickets, I had panels lined up, and I had a week of interactions and recordings to deliver.

And now I had a decision to make.

I looked down at the phone in my lap.

"Let's see what they're offering."

I opened the email, reading the contract terms.

New York. They wanted me to relocate to New-fucking-York. As in half a world away, New York. Everything I'd ever wanted hovered within my grasp.

"So why do I feel so fucking awful?"

I pinched the bridge of my nose, tears stinging my eyes.

"No more pity parties. You need to have a shower, get dressed, and deliver on your commitments." I turned my chair, catching sight of myself in the bungalow mirror.

Hair dishevelled, eyes swollen and bloodshot, nose a pink mess—I looked like the definition of 'break up.'

"And let's add an inch of makeup to the to-do list."
With a deep sigh, I began my day.

## 30

**Jay**

My malaise had returned with a side order of self-flagellation. Sprawled out on my bed, the last forty-eight hours felt less like reality and more like a horrible nightmare.

But it had happened. All of it.

I closed my eyes, replaying for the millionth time the exact moment I'd destroyed Frankie—her heart shattering while I watched.

A loud thud on my window interrupted my pity party. A second came a moment later, followed by a third, then a fourth.

"What the fuck?"

I contemplated remaining in bed but the regularity and increased frequency with which the pounding continued forced me up and out. I ripped back the curtains, squinting into the light to see—

"Toilet paper?"

I scrubbed a hand over my face blinking to clear my

vision. Yep, yards of toilet paper hung from every dinosaur and tree in my yard, and standing in the middle of the mess dressed in full black, their faces red and angry stood Mai, Annie, and Flo.

"Fuck."

I reached for my sweatpants, mentally girding my loins for their inevitable roasting.

"Not like I don't deserve it."

The thumps began again, pounding against my windows.

I yanked the door open, stepping into the sea of white. "Stop."

Annie glared at me, bouncing a toilet roll in one hand. "Absolutely not."

I blew out a breath. "Annie, seriously, stop. You didn't even like me with Frankie."

"What I like doesn't matter, you jerk-off. She wanted you. She *still* wants you. She saw something in you she felt deserves love. Did I want to give you that chance? Fuck no. But she did. And you fucked her over."

She pitched the toilet roll over the roof of my house, the paper unrolling in a glorious arch.

"I'll note I'm not involved in this display of childishness," Flo commented, one hand resting on Ace's head. "And if Frankie knew about this, she would be just as disapproving."

"I have no qualms." Mai lobbed her own roll at my triceratops family, managing to hit the Daddy-tops on the head. "We have an unlimited supply of toilet paper and a burning rage against men in our belly. You think this is bad? You have no idea."

I scrubbed a hand over my face. "She doesn't love me."

All three women stopped.

"You have got to be fucking kidding me."

"She just thinks she does," I said, my chest aching. "She'll get over it. She'll move on. She'll find the love of her life and go back to being the incredible woman she is."

Flo's hands fluttered, pressing against her chest. "And what about you?"

"What about him?" Mai snapped, hands on hips. "No one gives a—"

"Wait." Annie stared at me, a toilet roll clutched in her hand. "Jay, why do you think she doesn't love you?"

"I—" My throat closed, my chest tight. "You should go."

Mai sucked in a breath, her hand clutching Flo's.

"Jay." Annie stepped closer, her gaze searching my face. "Why do you think she doesn't love you?"

I closed my eyes, rubbing at the skin above my chest, McKenzie's words ringing in my ears.

*Do you really expect her to fall in love with you? You're a fuck boy, Jay. You know that.*

I opened my mouth trying to summon words, sounds, anything except the aching silence that seemed to be blocking my throat.

"You love her." Annie dropped the toilet roll. "Fuck. You really love her."

"I—" The denial died before it began. "Yeah, I do."

"Does she know you love her?"

I nodded glumly.

"Then why'd you do it?" Mai asked.

"Because she deserves better. She deserves the best." I waved a hand at my yard. "I'm the guy you come to for a fuck. I'm a good time. You think I don't know people call me Hot Jay? That's all the fuck they think I'm worth. And I'll be fucked if I drag her down with me."

The women were silent for a beat, then exploded, all of them moving toward me.

"Bullshit—!"

"What the fuck—?"

"How can you even think—"

I backed up as they trampled through my wrecked yard.

"Me first!" Annie yelled, thrusting her arms out to halt Mai and Flo's movements. She turned to me, her colour up, rage in her expression.

"You are a fucking idiot."

She stepped closer, hands on hips, her expression deadly.

"I'm not going to ask you to explain whatever the fuck issue is going on in your head because years of counselling is needed to help you with that mess. I will, however, ask you to explain what's in your heart."

I rubbed at my chest. "What heart?"

"God damn it, Jay!" She stabbed me in the chest with a finger. "I disliked you. I thought she was too good for you. I worried about her. I worried about her heart. But now?" She shook her head. "You're as fucked up about this as she is. Which only means one thing."

"What's that?"

"That you love her, stupid!" Flo burst out, her hands curving into fists. "And if you love her that means you belong together! Admit it, just fucking admit it!"

The wall around my emotions burst, the words flowing freely.

"Of course I fucking love her! She's Frankie. She's sweet, and sexy, and hilarious, and serious, and so fucking intelligent she blows my mind. She's creating a life for herself that is beyond anything I could ever imagine and what do I have to offer her? A fucking wreck of a home and a bunch of dinosaur statues. What am I? Fucking five? I'm not the guy she marries. I'm the guy she fucks and gets over."

"Do you want a future with her?" Mai asked, tears dancing on her lashes.

"Of course, I fucking do!"

"Then make it happen."

I blinked. "What?"

"Frankie isn't asking a lot. She doesn't expect you to be perfect." Mai gestured at herself and the women beside her. "She loves us because of our imperfections. She'll take you as you are, Jay. She'll do whatever's necessary to build a future with you. All she's asking for—all she wants, is for you to do the same."

I stared at the women, something shifting into place.

"Fuck." I ran a hand through my hair. "Fuck."

"Flo, his expression is what I would call stunned-male-suffering-from-idiotic-self-realization," Annie said, watching me.

"That's on brand. Do you think he'll decide to make a grand gesture now?"

"Jay," Mai said, her voice soft. "Before you do anything, you need to know, she's been offered a talk show in New York."

I doubled over, my breath escaping me. "Fuck." I closed my eyes. "That's her dream." My heart raced, my mind operating at a million miles an hour as I struggled to work out my next step.

"Is he okay?" Flo asked. "There's a lot of grunting."

"I don't know. He's bent over and turning red." Annie moved to my side, placing a hand on my shoulder. "Jay? Talk to us, bud. What's—"

I jerked upright. "When's her live podcast?" I barked, pegging Mai with a glare. "Quick!"

"T-t-today. This afternoon."

"What time?"

Annie pulled her cell from her pocket, scrolling down the screen. "It's at six."

"Shit. What's the time?"

"Just after nine, why?"

I did some rapid calculations. "If we leave now, we can make it."

"What?" three voices screeched, their faces pictures of surprise.

I turned to sprint inside, catching a whiff of myself on the way to my bedroom.

"Fuck!" I'd have to factor in shower time. But if we drove straight through, we could make it in—

"What are you doing?" Annie yelled from my porch.

"Planning a grand-fucking-gesture!"

## 31

## Frankie

"I'm sorry," I smiled politely at the organiser. "Did you say McKenzie Rylan?"

The harried woman nodded, chugging water like she had just crawled out of the desert.

I'd arrived at the hall where my podcast interview was to be held—only to find the support staff in disarray. The AC had failed at some point, leaving us in a damp, humid puddle of sweat. But that wasn't the worst part.

"Half the festival is down with food poisoning," the organiser bemoaned, opening another bottle. "Bad oysters. I don't know why people think eating something that looks like snot is a good idea."

I steered her back to the issue at hand. "I could run it myself. I don't need another person on stage with me."

"Oh, don't you worry. McKenzie volunteered. Bless her, she's such a darling." The woman's cell beeped, her face paling as she looked at the screen. "Oh God, not another one." She walked off, vowing loudly to never host another event.

"Well, shit," I muttered smoothing damp palms down my skirt. "This sucks."

"What does?"

My neck snapped around, finding McKenzie standing behind me. She wore a gorgeous Marilyn Monroe-esque white dress, her body showcased to perfection. How she hadn't broken a sweat in this heat I had no idea.

"That so many people have food poisoning," I lied.

She considered me, her lips pursing. "Mm. But their loss is our gain. I'm being paid overtime for these panels."

I forced a smile. "Us starving artists need every coin we can get."

She tilted her head to one side, looking at me as if I were an interesting bug she wanted to study. "You're not what I expected."

I didn't rise to the bait. "Did you want to run over some questions or lines before we start? I'm happy to discuss anything—"

"He left you, didn't he?"

I guess we were having this conversation.

"He did."

She nodded. "I knew he would. I'd hoped for better but...." She trailed off.

My aversion to conflict warred with my conscience—I knew I needed to say something but desperately wished I didn't have to be the one to say it to her.

The dead look in Jay's eyes hit me, flaring my anger.

*Fuck it. Let's do this.*

"McKenzie, before we go on stage there's something I need to say." I waited until she looked at me, her expression mildly curious.

"What you did to Jay was unacceptable. You hurt him all those years ago. Instead of being the bigger person, you took a coward's way out of a relationship. You hurt a man who only wanted to love you, and you continued to hurt him by planting seeds in him that should never have grown. Your actions the other night were reprehensible. For your sake and his—do better. You can still be a strong, independent woman without dragging others down."

My hands shook, adrenaline surging while I waited for her reaction.

She pursed her lips, a slight frown marring her forehead.

"I have never—"

The stage manager interrupted. "Frankie? McKenzie? We're ready for you."

I pushed away, heading for the two chairs set up in the middle of the stage. I could hear McKenzie walking behind me, her heels echoing on the wooden floor.

I transitioned to the allocated chair, the roadie returning to wheel Pinkie offstage.

"Frankie?"

I looked at the woman who'd broken the heart of the man I loved.

"It wasn't personal."

"Not to you," I told her. "But it was to him. Actions have consequences—and for Jay, that consequence lasted years."

She stared at me then abruptly looked away. "You ready?"

I released a silent sigh. "Whenever you are."

She lifted her microphone, switching it on. "Hello, lovely listeners! I'm McKenzie Rylan and it is my absolute pleasure to be interviewing the wonderful Doctor Frankie Kenton."

Surprisingly, the next hour went quickly. McKenzie

settled into her role as facilitator, prompting me on different issues and aspects of my show and my work.

I kind of hated that I didn't hate it.

"And that's all we have time for today," McKenzie said, wrapping up the discussion. "Thank you so much for joining us for the live recording, Frankie."

I offered her a genuine smile. "Thanks for having me. "

"That concludes our streaming portion. For those who are here in person, we'll now take questions. Please make your way in an orderly fashion to the allocated microphones."

If not for the ache in my heart, I would have called this a good day. Maybe even a best day as the audience burst into applause, lines already forming at the microphones. I'd packed the auditorium, thousands of fans crammed into the conference space all coming to listen to me.

It should have been a best day but without Jay, it felt... empty.

"And now for questions." McKenzie waved at one of the lines. "Yes, you."

"Hi, Frankie, I'm Gemma, a long-time listener and absolute fan." The girl danced from side to side, her grin a mix of nervous excitement. "I just wanted to say without you I'd have never gotten up the courage to kiss the person who became my boyfriend."

The crowd broke into applause, the guy standing and giving a little wave.

"We listen to your show together and learn something new every time. I wanted to thank you, it's opened the door for better communication in our relationship."

"Thank you," I said, my heart in my throat. "I love that for both of you."

"My question is which is your favourite episode and why?"

My stomach dropped, nausea flooding my mouth. I forced myself to answer, determined to be honest.

"If you'd asked me three months ago, I'd have said the profile on stimulating the brain. But recently I met someone who taught me about rope, and—" I coughed, struggling to speak around the lump in my throat. "And he helped me find a part of myself I didn't know was missing. The three episodes on ropes and accessible play are my new favourites."

The questions came thick and fast, everything from my favourite sex toy to which politician I'd be voting for—nothing seemed taboo.

"And that's all the time we have for questions today. If you'll join me in thanking—"

"Wait!"

The interruption came from the far back of the auditorium. I lifted my hand, squinting against the bright stage lights. The crowd shifted, parting for four people and a familiar dog as they sprinted down the aisle toward one of the microphones.

"Wait! I have a question."

My heart skipped as I stared at the man who'd broken my heart.

Jay looked like shit—his suit crumpled, his hair a mess. And yet he also looked like the best thing I'd ever seen.

He stumbled to a halt at the microphone, ripping it free of the stand.

"I'm sorry," McKenzie said, her tone brisk. "You'll have to take it offline. We've finished question time. Ms. Kenton has to—"

"I'll take his question," I blurted, my heart in my throat. "Go ahead."

Mai, Annie, and Flo stopped behind Jay, all of them bent over as they sucked in deep gulps of air. The only one who didn't seem winded was Ace, the dog sitting at the ready beside Flo.

"Doctor Kenton," Jay began, his gaze locking with mine. "What would you say to someone who sees themselves only as dispensable?"

I swallowed, forcing moisture into my parched mouth. "I'd say they're worth so much more than they think. But I could speak until I'm blue in the face, if they don't believe in themself then there's not much of a point in having the conversation."

"But what if they're learning to believe?" Jay asked, taking a step toward the stage. "What if they're trying really hard to let go of decades of shit and see themselves in a new light?"

"Then I'd say welcome to the club, and I'm glad you're seeking help. We all have baggage, it's whether we hold on to, process, or leave it behind that matters."

He kept moving, the crowd shifting as he walked down the aisle toward me. I could see the dark circles under his eyes, the slightly too-long beard, the anxious tension in his shoulders. I itched to soothe fingers over his frown lines, ached to make a joke to ease the tension around his eyes. But he wasn't mine, not any more.

"Would you date someone willing to try? Even though they're a mess? Even though they've fucked up? Would you be willing to take a chance on someone trying to fix themselves?"

I stared at him. "Friendship date?"

He shook his head. "Marriage date. Love date. Forever and always date."

A little piece of my shattered heart reattached, hope binding it together. "What are you asking?"

He sucked in a breath, stopping in front of the stage, his beautiful green eyes unwavering as he stared at me.

"Frankie Kenton, I love you."

Gasps rocked the auditorium.

"I can't imagine life without you. I couldn't even get through twenty-four hours. You're my raptor, Frankie. You're my sunshine, my rainbow, my hero, my pot of gold." He placed the microphone on the edge of the stage, boosting himself up to stride across the raised platform, stopping in front of me.

"I love you. Please forgive me."

Heart full, I looked behind him to where Annie, Flo, and Mai stood. Annie gave me a thumbs-up, while Mai nodded encouragingly. They both leaned in to whisper in Flo's ears. Flo grinned, placing a hand over her heart, giving her blessing.

I looked back at Jay, seeing my own heartache reflected back at me.

"Jay?"

"Yes, rainbow?"

"Say it again."

"I'm sorry."

I shook my head. "No, the other thing."

"I love you."

I nodded, savouring the words. "And again."

"I love you."

"One more time?"

He grinned, tipping his head back to yell, "I love you!"

I laughed, lifting up a hand to crook my finger at him. He came, dropping to his knees and shuffling forward until he could wrap me in his arms.

"I love you," he whispered, searching my face. "And I'm fucking sorry I let doubts threaten what we have."

"Promise not to white-fang me again?"

He laughed, nodding.

"Promise to talk to me? I'm serious, none of this walking out bullshit." I pressed a hand to my heart. "I couldn't do it again."

"I fucking promise."

"Then kiss me like you mean it."

He caught my mouth and I expected a hungry claiming —but I should have known Jay would surprise me. His hand came up, tangling in my hair, his other wrapping around my back. He pressed slow, featherlight kisses to my lips, my mouth falling open under his sensual onslaught.

"Um, well, that's, what I mean to say is—" McKenzie cleared her throat. "This concludes today's session with Doctor Frankie Kenton from the *All Access* podcast. And a reminder Frankie will be on the panel tomorrow to discuss sexual trauma, and she'll be hosting a second show on Friday discussing sex worker rights. We hope you've enjoyed today's event and don't forget to check out the merch desk on your way out."

I pressed my forehead to Jay's. "We should probably find a room."

"Yeah. Though it might be difficult considering I didn't exactly come alone." He glanced over his shoulder at my cheering friends. "And I think Mai will only forgive me if I put them up in the penthouse for the night."

I giggled, giving him a little squeeze. "If you ask nicely, I might let you stay with me."

"Rainbow." He kissed me again. "It's cute you think you had a choice." He pulled back. "Where's your wheelchair?"

I pointed at the far side of the stage.

"You gonna protest if I carry you?"

My heart did a strange skipping thing.

"You could just bring it over."

"I could." He shifted, sliding his arms under my knees, one hand behind my back. "But then you wouldn't be in my arms."

He hefted me up, staggering a little as I wrapped my arms around his neck.

"You alright there, champ?" I laughed. "Sure you can carry me?"

He grinned. "Baby, I'll carry you to the ends of the fucking earth."

Secure in his arms, he strode across the stage "I Need a Hero" under his breath.

And I loved every minute.

## 32

**Jay**

I'd managed to ditch Flo, Mai, and Annie by handing them my credit card and telling them to have fun. They'd headed for the closest bar, ready for a night out on my dime.

Considering I had a half-naked Frankie under me I'd say it was a worthwhile investment.

"I'm sorry," I muttered, stroking hands down her sides. "I should have stayed."

"Mm," she murmured. "You really should have."

We kissed, long and slow, our tongues stroking, our bodies pressing together tightly.

"But will you next time?" she asked, shifting to allow me to remove her dress.

"Absolutely. Lesson has been learned." I paused in my seduction effort to pull my cell free from my back pocket, navigating to the calendar app to show her. "I booked an appointment with a psychologist. I need to learn how to process the shit from my past."

"Oh, God." Frankie pressed a hand to her chest. "I just realised I have an emotionally intelligent man fetish."

I grinned, tossing the cell onto the side table and reached for her dress. "Would it surprise you to learn I've been speaking to your friends who counselled me on vulnerability and shame for the full six-hour drive?"

"No. My friends adore me, and they're all disciples of our queen and emotional saviour, Brené Brown."

I nuzzled her neck. "Why does this feel like a situation where you'll make me watch a TED Talk?"

"Later." She laughed. "And I'll buy you some books."

"I adore you."

"Then prove it." She halted my movement. "Go check in the box by the door."

"Is it a present for me?" I asked, jumping off the bed to go scavenge.

"No, it's a present for me."

I tossed my shirt on a chair as I passed, my hands dropping to unzip my fly. I shoved off my pants, kicking them away, then crouched, ripping open the big box.

"What is it?" I pulled out a bunch of different-sized cushions, some wedge-shaped, some rectangles, and one in the shape of a doughnut. "Are these what I think they are?"

Frankie's chuckle sent all the blood in my body racing to my dick.

"Yep. They're sex props." She gave a sexy little shimmy. "Wanna try them out?"

"Fuck yes."

I hauled the props across the room, tossing them on the bed before heading to the bathroom to wash my hands. I returned to find Frankie naked on the bed, her fingers spreading herself wide.

"Fuck me, you're gorgeous," I growled, desperate for a taste.

"Like what you see?" she asked, her index finger tracing her clit.

I reached down to fist my cock. "Fuck, yes."

I returned to the bed, moving to cover her body with mine. Nipping at her earlobe, my hands crept up to unclip her bra. "I'm going to make love to you until the memories of the last two days are wiped clean."

She sighed, melting under me. "I love that you set goals every time we make love."

"Gotta make sure we're clear on the outcomes."

"Mm, maybe I should do the same?"

"What would your goal be?"

I could see her thinking as I pulled her bra free, my head dipping to suck first one nipple, then the other, running my beard along her sensitive skin.

"How about, I'm gonna make love to you until you can't think of anyone but me."

I snorted. "It's nice to see you're setting yourself attainable goals. Congratulations, you achieved it weeks ago."

"I cannot believe you're making fun of me." Her hands ran down my back to grip my ass. "But because you have an amazing body, I'll forgive you."

I chuckled, peppering kisses across her gorgeous curves, my hands guiding my way.

"Fuck," I muttered, peeling off her soaked underwear and finding her thighs wet with arousal. "Fuck, fuck, fuck."

"You okay down there?"

With one hand I shifted the wedges, positioning them beside her. With the other I found her piercing, playing with the small barbell.

"God," Frankie groaned, tipping her head back, hands clenching the bed sheets. "Keep going."

"No. I wanna fuck you from behind."

Frankie blinked her eyes open, a small smile creeping across her lips. "I thought you'd never ask."

I helped her move, watching her position herself, helping to adjust her legs.

"Wait," she said, reaching behind her to place a hand on my stomach, preventing me from getting any closer. "Jay, I need help up here."

*Fuck.*

I moved up the bed, shifting to her head. "What's wrong?"

"Can you just—" She laid a hand on my thigh, guiding me to kneel directly in front of her head. "—there, perfect."

"What do you—fuck!" Curses spilled from my lips as her lips closed around my cock, her hand dropping to my balls. "And you call me evil."

She glanced up, grinning around my dick.

"Complaints?" she asked, pulling back to tongue the crown of my cock.

"Fuck no."

I shifted, giving her a better angle to work me over, her hot mouth pushing me to the edge of my control.

"Babe, stop."

She made a sound of denial.

"Rainbow, stop." I pulled away, Frankie protesting.

I tangled fingers in her hair, gently but firmly peeling her greedy mouth from my cock. "I said no."

She blinked up at me, her lips turning down in a pout. "But—"

"No." I ran hands down her back until I could palm her

ass. "I'm gonna fuck your tight pussy and you're gonna fucking love it."

Her hair brushed my stomach, her body shuddering under my hands.

"Jay."

My name on her tongue ruined me. I spanked her ass, then shifted around the bed to settle between her legs. I leaned forward, my teeth grazing her shoulder, nipping then kissing away the sting.

I snatched a condom from the bedside table, rolling it on as one hand ran up her thigh, finding her slit and beginning to play. Condom sorted, I gathered her hair, holding her in place.

"Tell me you love me."

Frankie whimpered. "I love you."

I began to fuck her with my fingers. "Tell me you need me."

"Please," she moaned. "I need you, Jay. I need your cock in me. I need you to fuck my tight pussy."

A harsh sound ripped from my throat, need riding me hard.

I dropped my hand from her, fisting my cock and guiding myself to her core, rubbing against her, coating myself in the evidence of her desire.

"The first time I saw you." I dragged my cock over her clit, rubbing and teasing us both. "I wanted your mouth. I wanted you to feel and touch every part of me."

I ran my tongue from the low of her back up to the curve of her neck, nuzzling her cheek.

"You, my sweet Frankie, blew every fantasy I had out of the water. Hot, wet, and fucking incredible, I want more." I fucked into her, sheathing my cock in one hard move, loving her breathy moan.

Seated deep in her, my hands brushed the sensitive curve of her hips, her filthy moans testing my control.

"I need more," she panted, her hands gripping the headboard, using it to move her body. "More, Jay. More."

I gave her a shallow thrust. "Like that?"

"More."

I moved again, just a little. "How's that one?"

"Jay!"

I gripped her hips, holding her still while I thrust into her—hard, fast, and rough.

"Yes!" she breathed, hands now braced against the headboard. "More, more, more. Jay!"

Our bodies met in a wet, harsh clash, her pussy a hot grip around my dick.

I grunted praises and curses, muttering filthy sentences as I drove into her, desperate to build her orgasm.

"Come for me," I demanded harshly, reaching down to finger her clit. "Give it to me, Frankie. Fuck my cock. Milk me, rainbow. Fuck my—"

She shattered, her body's tight squeeze tipping me over the edge. I made love to her until we both collapsed in a wet, sticky, panting mess. I rolled onto the bed beside her, one hand resting on her ass, my body ruined.

"Jay?" Frankie panted, her eyes closed tight, body slumped over the wedges.

"Mm?"

"Kiss me."

I jacked up, scooping her into my arms and gently moving us until she could snuggle in my arms, our lips meeting for a long, lazy kiss.

"Rainbow, I need to tell you something."

She tilted her head back, our gazes holding.

"You should take the New York job."

"How did you—?"

"Your friends mentioned it."

She rolled her eyes. "They're terrible at keeping secrets."

I ran my hands through her hair, holding her in place. "We'll make it work. New York, Capricorn Cove, Australia—wherever you are, I'm going to be. These are your dreams and I want you to pursue them. Whatever you need, rainbow, you tell me."

"Well." A small smile teased her lips. "I might need a room in your house. And some bookshelves. And the occasional trip to New York."

"Frankie, what are you saying?"

"The show they pitched me will have limited run seasons—fifteen episodes and they record three episodes a day. Which means—" She leaned in, nipping at my earlobe. "You're stuck with me."

"Fuck, I love you." I burned, aching with gratitude and awe for this woman.

She sighed, burrowing into me. "I know."

Amusement wound through me. "You know, hmm?"

"I knew the minute you destroyed a wall to make room in your house for me."

I froze, thinking back. "Well, shit."

She giggled, her lips finding my collarbone. "You can't hide from me, Jay Wood. I see you."

I buried my hands in her hair, tipping her head back to stare into her beautiful blue eyes. "Thank God."

And with that, I kissed the woman I wanted to spend the rest of my life loving.

# EPILOGUE ONE

**Jay**

*Six months later*

The letter arrived on an ordinary Tuesday. Frankie had placed it on our entry table, leaning it against one of her five Poddie awards. I picked it up, making a mental note to polish her Podcast of the Year statue.

"What's this?" I asked, wandering into the kitchen. Dressed in leggings and a baggy jersey I'd worn in high school, she looked as delicious as the dinner she was making smelled.

"Looks like a letter to me."

I bent, giving her a hello kiss. "Mm, you smell like red sauce."

"And you are filthy." She laughed, pushing me away. "How on earth did you get so dirty?"

"We got a call from the rangers to help clear some trees that came down in the last storm." I sighed dreamily. "Picture it, Frankie. Big old redwoods, perfectly aged. I'm gonna make the most magnificent furniture with those babies. They're gonna have the best afterlife."

She snorted, smacking me on the butt as she moved past me, reaching for the salt. "Does that include making me the desk of my dreams?"

"Maybe." I didn't tell her, but I'd already completed her desk, it sat in my workshop waiting for her birthday next week.

I turned the letter over in my hands. "It's from McKenzie." I traced a thumb over her name on the return address. "Why would she be writing to me?"

Frankie sprinkled the salt across the top of the happily bubbling sauce, mixing it in. "We could speculate or you could open it and find out."

I rolled my eyes. "You're no fun."

"That's not what you were saying last night."

My cock thickened at the reminder of Frankie sitting on the swing I'd rigged in our bedroom, her body bound, her face a picture of ecstasy as I pressed a vibrator against her clit.

"Low blow. Maybe we should—"

"Jay, open the damn letter."

With a long sigh, I slid my finger through the envelope, pulling the note free.

"Dear Jay," I read aloud. "It's taken me some time to write this note to you. These words aren't easy to say but they're necessary."

I stopped reading, stuck on the next sentence.

"You okay?"

I nodded. "She says she's sorry."

"For?"

I scanned the rest of the letter's contents. "For everything. The cheating, the lying, the bullshit she fed me." I shook my head. "This is unexpected."

"But welcome?"

"I don't know. It feels like...." I trailed off, realisation slamming into me.

"Like?" Frankie repeated, tossing the spoon in the sink and turning her wheelchair to face fully toward me.

"Like she has no hold over me. I appreciate her apology and I'm glad she's getting help but—" I shrugged. "She doesn't have a place in my life. Her opinion doesn't influence my happiness."

Frankie crooked her finger and I leaned down, closing my eyes when she cupped my cheeks, her lips peppering little kisses all over my face.

"Proud of you."

I let her words sink deep, memorising this moment.

"Rainbow?"

"Mm?"

"Will you—"

The red sauce chose that moment to boil over, the acrid smell of burnt food filling the kitchen.

I jumped to save it but smoke billowed from the pot, the evidence clear—dinner was ruined.

"No!" Frankie cried, laughing as I dumped the pot in the sink. "I thought I had it this time."

"Babe, we need to make peace with you being a disaster in the kitchen."

"Worst girlfriend ever."

On the kitchen floor with the smell of burnt sauce in the air, I dropped to one knee. "How about we ditch the girlfriend title? Marry me?"

Her eyes widened, her mouth forming a little O.

"Are you—?"

I nodded. "Marry me, Frankie. Let's tie this relationship up. Let's make this permanent."

She let out a startled, strangled laugh. "Oh, God. But I burnt dinner."

"I know." I grinned. "That's why God created takeout menus."

"Yes! A million, billion, trillion times yes, yes, yes!"

I reached out, flicking her footrests up and placing her feet gently on the ground. I moved in, wrapping my arms around her, gratified when she did the same.

"I love you."

She sighed, holding me tighter. "Love you too."

I shifted, pressing our foreheads together. "Don't make me wait too long."

She laughed and I kissed her, my tongue sweeping into her mouth, tasting the joy on her tongue.

"Wait." She put a hand to my chest, pushing me back an inch. "Do I have to change my name?"

"And go from Francine Ursula Charles Kenton, Doctor FUCK to Doctor Wood?" I snorted. "Hell no. I'll change mine."

She blinked. "You'd take my name?"

"Of course."

She flushed, a pleased grin stealing across her face. "You're making me rethink my no anal rule."

I chuckled, pulling her back into my chest, holding her tight. "I'll keep working on my pitch."

She held one hand up, pretending to snap a picture of us.

"What's that for?"

She leaned into me. "It's a best day. And best days deserve to be remembered."

My chest felt tight, my heart too full of emotion. "Rainbow, I promise, this is just the start of our best days."

# EPILOGUE TWO

**Frankie**

"Do you think they're going to hook up?" I asked Mai, watching Annie and Lincoln as they argued at the bar.

"Almost definitely."

Flo sighed, crossing her arms over her chest. "Describe it to me."

"Her bridesmaid dress has slipped a little, revealing more cleavage than I think she's aware," I said, watching with great amusement as Linc's gaze dipped.

"If only the rest of us were so amply blessed," Mai bemoaned, cupping her itty-bitty-titties. "I should get a boob job."

"Hush," Flo hissed. "Tell me more."

"Linc's glaring at the bartender and he—yep, he's ripped up the guy's number and—" I bit out a laugh. "Flo, he's thrown her over his shoulder and is now walking out."

"I'm surprised Annie hasn't started scream—"

"WHAT THE FUCK ARE YOU DOING?" Annie's screech cut through the reception, conversation ceasing as heads of the loitering waitstaff twisted their way. "This is my best friend's wedding, motherfucker! And you're ruining it!"

Linc turned, his hand resting on a squirming Annie's ass.

"Frankie, Jay. Best wishes to you both but we're gonna bail." He bounced Annie on his shoulder. "This one is drunk and needs to get home."

I opened my mouth to protest but Mai beat me to the punch.

"Annie, we'll call you tomorrow. Have fun!"

She screeched, her tirade cut off by the close of the heavy banquet door.

"I'm putting money down right now—they never got over each other," Flo declared, looking exceptionally pleased. "I predict another wedding within the year."

"Please God, no. Can you imagine an Annie wedding?" Mai groaned, one arm flopping over her eyes. "Frankie's dress nearly killed me."

I looked down at the sexy number, loving the intricate bodice that made me look like a freaking queen. I smoothed a hand over the beautiful silk skirt, sighing again at the soft fabric under my palm.

"You nailed it. This mermaid is gorgeous."

"I know. But Annie's?" She shook her head. "She'll want a princess ball gown with lace and sparkle and satin and a top that makes her breasts look as if Zeus himself is cupping them."

"And pockets," Flo added, her tongue flicking out to capture the last of the icing from our cake. "Don't forget the pockets."

I raised my glass. "To Mai and her hardworking fingers."

"To Frankie and Jay, and their beautiful love story," Flo said, holding her own drink aloft.

"To the open bar!" Mai said, thrusting her glass into the air.

We clinked our flutes together, drinking the bubbling champagne.

"Ladies, I hate to interrupt." Jay draped an arm over my shoulders, tipping my head back to steal a breathtaking kiss. "But I need to steal my wife for the final dance."

I allowed him to lead me, laughing when he positioned me in the middle of the makeshift floor.

"Jay, what are you doing?" I gestured at the near-empty room. "The band is packing up."

"Stay here."

The reception had wrapped up a half hour ago, but I'd wanted a little time with our closest friends to say thank you for all their hard work before leaving for our honeymoon.

"I have one last surprise to get you ready for the wedding night."

The lights in the venue dimmed, leaving only the dance floor lit as he walked away from me, striking a pose at the far end of the room.

"What is happening right now?" I asked, exchanging a bemused look with Mai who was describing the scene to Flo, Jay's groomsmen crowding in beside them.

"I don't know," she called laughter in her voice. "You're the one who married him!"

Jay nodded at the lead singer of the band. The guy sent him a thumbs-up, hitting a button on his sound desk, music pumping through the speakers around the room.

"Is this... 'Pony'?" I asked, staring at my husband.

Jay began to move, his hips gyrating in time to the Ginuwine song. His body bent and flexed as he shrugged off his jacket, threw off his tie. Then on with a run, he dropped to his knees and slid across the floor to stop directly in front of my chair, ripping his shirt free, buttons flying.

"Oh my God," I whispered, simultaneously horrified and impressed by his striptease.

He executed a perfect body roll from the floor to a stand, moving like a fluid wave as he bent, brushing a soft kiss against my lips.

"Hey there, sexy lady."

Before I could grab him, he twirled, dropping to the floor to grind his hips down.

"Why have you never used that on me in the bedroom?" I asked, laughing.

He sent me a wink. "Gotta save some moves for tonight."

I lost it, tears of laughter spilling down my cheeks as he performed a complicated worm, bouncing up to a stand, immediately tossing a leg over my chair to perform explicit hip thrusts in my face, his cock bouncing suggestively against his tight trousers.

"Oh, God," I cried, pressing my hands to my face. "Why did you think this was a good idea?"

The song began to build to a climax, Jay whipping my chair around to swing me this way and that, his body a constant movement of thrusts, grinds, and shimmying until his pants slipped down his legs as the song finished, leaving him bent over in front of my chair, a sassy look on his face as he glanced at me over his shoulder, his ass clad only in—

"Are those *dinosaur* boxers?" I choked, succumbing to my laughter.

Jay stood, turning to spread his arms wide, his grin massive as he panted, catching his breath. "It seemed only right."

I crooked my finger and he immediately leaned in, kissing me.

"You are an idiot," I said between gales of laughter and kisses. "You're lucky I love you."

He caught my hand, running his finger over the giant ring. "Is this a best day?"

I slid a hand across his chest to press it against his racing heart. "Abso-fucking-lutely."

He laughed. "Shall we get out of here and get this marriage started?"

"Did you pack the ropes?"

His grin stretched from one side of his face to the other. "Of course."

"You sure you're ready to tie me down?" I teased.

"Rainbow, there's nothing in the world that could stop me."

With a final kiss to seal his promise, we began our happily ever after.

**Thank you so much for reading Knot My Type!**
**The All Access series continues with Love Flushed which is available right now!**

**Be sure to visit my website and use the code EBOOK10 to receive 10% off your next ebook purchase.**
**www.EvieMitchell.com**

# LEARN MORE

For those who may like more information about disability, the Australian Network on Disability has an inclusive language guide and excellent resources on their website.

The website Shibari study also has great resources for anyone seeking more information.

# ACKNOWLEDGMENTS

There are so many people I would like to thank for this book. Firstly, to everyone who shared, read, reviewed, and commented on Knot My Type. Thank you from the bottom to the top of my heart. You are incredible and I am so thankful for every single one of you.

To Erin, Yakari, and Kirsten my beautiful expert readers and friends. You have gone above and beyond to ensure this book represented Frankie, Mai, Ren, and all the other characters with love and integrity. I appreciate you.

To Nina, Bec, and Liliana. Thank you for your overwhelming support, love, and generosity. You are what makes life wonderful.

To my incredible beta readers—thank you Karen, Ashley, Janeane, Danni, and Kristina. You kept me sane and killed it. This book would be nothing without you.

To Lea and Mel (Alexa Riley), who invited me on the Read Me Romance podcast. That invite took me outside my comfort zone and forced me to write this book. Thank you so much!

To Eileen, my cover artist who took Frankie and Jay out of my head and brought them to life. You're the BEST!

And finally, to my incredible husband. You did housework, put up with me stressing, picked up the slack and were generally the most incredible person. I love you, thank you for being my happily ever after.

# BOOKS BY EVIE MITCHELL

**Larsson Sibling Series**

Thunder Thighs

Clean Sweep

The X-List

Reality Check

The Christmas Contract

**Capricorn Cove Series**

Double the D

Muffin Top

The Mrs. Clause

Beach Party

New Year Knew You

The Shake-Up

Double Breasted

As You Wish

You Sleigh Me

Resolution Revolution

Meat Load

**The Dogg Pack**

Puppy Love

The Frock Up

Pier Pressure

Bad English

**Nameless Souls MC Series**

Runner

Wrath

Ghost

Shield

**Elliot Security Series**

Rough Edge

Bleeding Edge

# CONNECT WITH EVIE MITCHELL

Facebook
Greedy Readers Book Club
TikTok
Instagram
Bookbub
Goodreads
Newsletter

Printed in the USA
CPSIA information can be obtained
at www.ICGtesting.com
LVHW042145150823
755380LV00026B/575

9 781922 561213